The Missing Comatose Woman

SARAH ETTRITCH

NORN PUBLISHING

TORONTO, CANADA

Library and Archives Canada Cataloguing in Publication

Ettritch, Sarah, 1963–
The missing comatose woman / Sarah Ettritch.

ISBN 978-1-927369-09-8

I. Title.

PS8609.T87M57 2013   C813'.6   C2013-900988-4

Editing by Marg Gilks
Cover design by Boulevard Photografica/Patty G. Henderson

v1

Published by Norn Publishing
www.NornPublishing.com

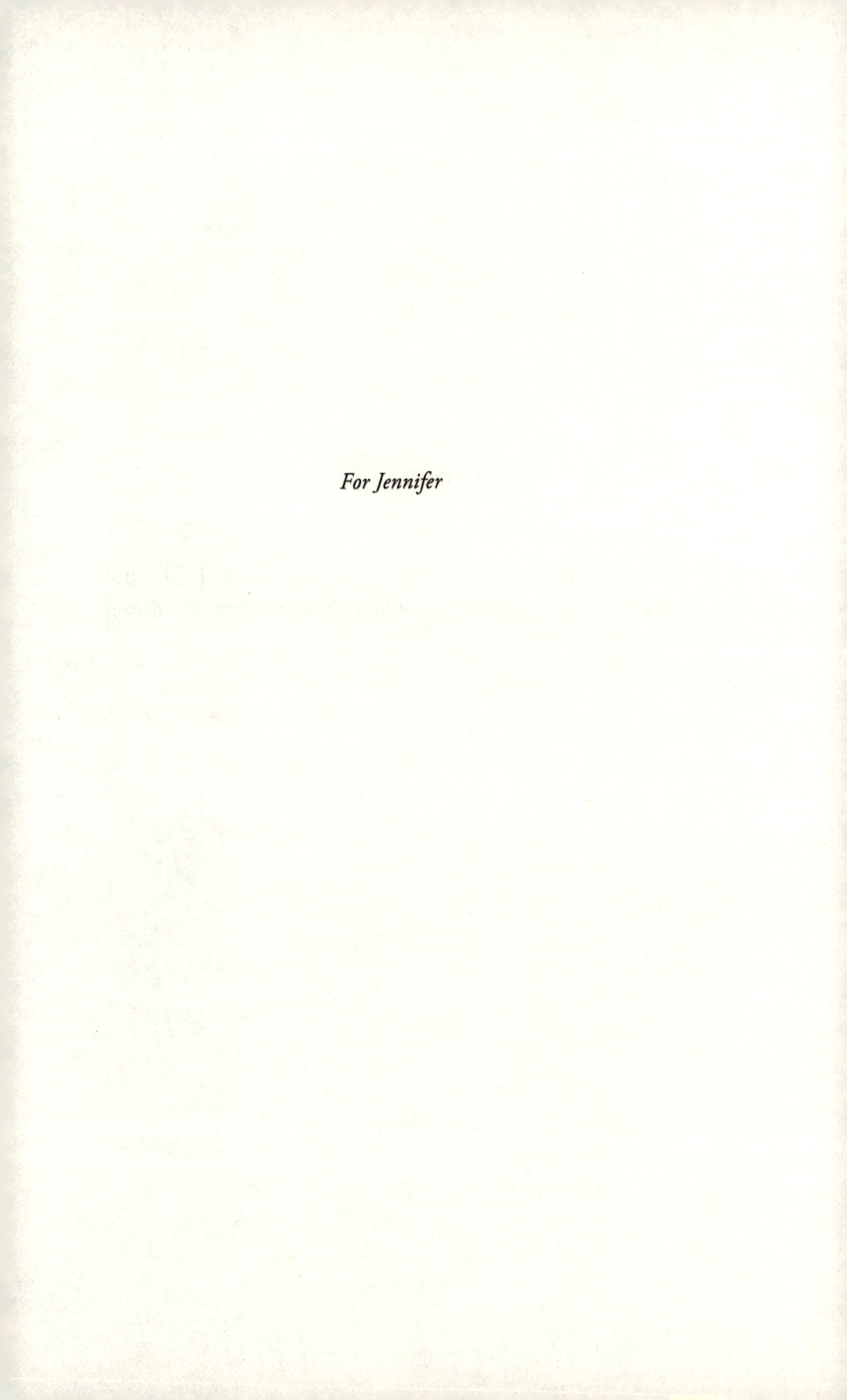

For Jennifer

Acknowledgements

My thanks to Jennifer Brinkman (my lovely partner and wonderful beta reader), Marg Gilks (my fabulous editor), and Patty Henderson (my talented cover designer).

Chapter One

ELLEN MYERS WATCHED the numbers change as the elevator rumbled its way up to the sixth floor. God, she hated hospitals; they made her itch. Couldn't the elevator go any faster? When the doors finally opened at her floor, she squeezed out of the elevator, scratched her arm, and tried not to touch anything. Everyone always said that if you didn't want to get sick, stay away from hospitals. But how could she, with Mom lying in a coma?

For the past month, Ellen had wolfed down her sandwich and yogurt, hopped into her car, and driven the ten minutes to Downtown General. She'd babble to Mom for fifteen minutes, race back to her car, and be back at her desk promptly at 1:00. Nobody could accuse her of slacking off because of "family troubles." Bastards.

She slowed as she approached Room 622. What would she say today? Could Mom hear her? Was she aware, only trapped inside an unresponsive body, or was Ellen talking to herself? How much longer would this go on? Every time she cornered the doctor for ten seconds, he bleated the same words: "No change. Still optimistic. Keep talking to her. Your visits are important." Her vision blurred. No, she had to be strong for Mom, breeze into that room and tell Mom all about her wonderful weekend at the spa. She'd leave out that she'd sniffled into her drinks.

Forcing a smile and squaring her shoulders, Ellen strode through the doorway chirping, "It's a lovely day today, Mom. I have lots to tell—"

She frowned, backed out of the room, and looked at the silver plate screwed next to the doorframe: *622*. Heart pounding, she walked into the room again and blinked at the empty, neatly made bed.

CASEY COOK CARRIED two glasses of lemonade into the living room and handed one to Gran. "Thank you," Gran mumbled, taking her glass without looking away from the TV. Sipping her own drink, Casey sank into the armchair and scowled at the screen, wishing she could turn down the volume as the audience roared with laughter at some joke a charismatic afternoon talk show guest had cracked.

Would she ever find a paying gig? She'd put up a website that promoted her services, but only bots and spammers had visited. Her friends were keeping their eyes and ears open for her, but half of them hadn't hidden their dismay when she'd left her job at Walmart to study for her private investigator licence, and the other half were just better actors. Casey hadn't doubted her choice, until now. She no longer daydreamed about landing eager clients and deftly handling whatever investigations came her way. Reality was a bitch.

The phone sitting on the coffee table rang.

"What?" Gran snapped.

Casey snatched up her phone and set the glass down in its place. "It's the phone."

"What?"

"The phone!" Casey bellowed, holding it up for Gran to see.

"Oh."

"Turn your damn hearing aids on," Casey said, knowing Gran couldn't hear her and would ignore her, if she could. If Casey didn't love the old bird, she would have killed her by now. She went into her bedroom and shut the door. "Hello."

"Casey Cook?" a woman said.

"Um, speaking."

"Oh, thank god! I was talking to a friend and she said maybe you could help me because you've helped a couple of people before and—"

"Slow down, slow down." Casey plunked onto the bed. Midnight uncurled and shot her a dirty look. "Sorry," she mouthed to the cat.

The woman on the other end sucked in a couple of deep breaths. "My mother is missing. A friend said you might be able to find her."

"I've helped people find their missing pets," Casey said as she stroked Mid. "I've never found a missing person before." As soon as the words were out of her mouth, she kicked herself. Telling prospective clients that she was inexperienced would never land her a case. Every private investigator had started out with a zero in the found persons column, right? "But that doesn't mean—"

"Look, I'm desperate. My mother's been missing for over a month. You've got to help me!"

Casey suppressed a whoop. It looked like her spanking new PI licence was about to see some action. "Why don't we meet and talk about it, Ms. . . . uh—"

"Myers. Ellen Myers. I can swing by your office after work. What's the address?"

Shit. If she didn't tell the truth, it would come back to bite her. "I usually meet clients at a local coffee shop." Okay, half the truth. After meeting Myers, it would be the truth.

"Oh. Sure. Diane said you were just starting out."

"Diane?"

"Jenkins."

"Jenkins?" Casey echoed, not sure she'd heard Myers correctly.

"Yes."

Considering that Diane had tried to persuade her not to "waste her time" studying for the licensing exam, she was the last friend Casey had expected would recommend her services. "How far away are you from Third and Jones?"

"Not far at all. I can be in that area by quarter after five."

"I'll wait for you outside the coffee shop on the northeast corner. I'll be wearing . . ." A trench coat and fedora? No. "Jeans and a gray hoodie. Brown hair. Slim."

"I wish I could say I was slim," Myers wailed. "I'll be the anxious woman with desperation in her eyes. God, I hope you can help me. See you later." The line went dead.

Casey slipped the phone into her pocket and wondered if she'd dreamed the call. Self-doubt quickly killed her euphoria. Oh god, she'd have to review her notes about missing person investigations. Not only that, in her excitement, she'd forgotten to discuss her fee.

What if Myers balked? What if Casey couldn't find her mother? She stared at her reflection in the dresser mirror. *Private investigator, my ass.*

Mid blinked at her. "Yeah, I know, I know. What the hell was I thinking, getting a PI licence? So I have a knack for finding missing cats, so what?" Instead of spending her time studying for her licence, maybe she should have thrown posters up around town advertising herself as some sort of pet locator, or contacted people who'd lost pets. Nah, that would have been preying on distraught owners, something she'd never do. She wanted people with missing pets to contact her.

Come on, you can do this. Everyone must have been nervous about their first case, right? Imagine telling her friends—especially Diane—that she'd given up before she'd started. *Yeah, after spending all the time and money on getting my licence, I thought, meh, not my thing. I didn't need to actually work on a case to figure it out. Sometimes you just know.* Jesus, after listening to her babble for hours on end about her future as a hotshot PI, they'd never speak to her again. "Do you realize what this means?" she said to Mid. "More toys that you'll play with once and never touch again!"

Her nervousness couldn't stifle her exuberance as she bounded down the hallway and into the living room. "I have a case, Gran. An honest to goodness case!"

Gran squinted at her. "Why do you need it?"

"What?"

"The suitcase."

"No. A case. A missing person," Casey said, enunciating every word.

Gran chortled. "Someone's taking a chance on you, eh?"

"Yes, someone's taking a chance."

"I hope they know they just hired the best damn private investigator in the country."

Casey plopped down next to Gran, squeezed her shoulders, and kissed her cheek. "And the investigator with the best damn grandmother."

CASEY SLIPPED THE photo of Jacqueline Rose, Myers' mother, between the pages of her pocket notebook and sipped her coffee. "So, you just arrived one day and your mother was gone?"

"Yes." Myers ripped open her third sugar packet and emptied its contents into her tea.

"And she was in a coma."

Myers glanced at Casey's notes.

"I have it all down." She'd merely wanted to confirm that she would, indeed, be looking for a person in a coma who'd apparently vanished. "What did you do when you realized she was gone?"

"I went to the nursing station. I figured they'd taken her away for a test, even though they knew I turned up every day at the same time. As soon as I arrived at the station, they were all, 'Oh, Ms. Myers, you must have forgotten. Your brother transferred your mother to a long-term care home.'"

"I take it he didn't," Casey said.

"He couldn't. I don't have a flipping brother!" Myers gulped down some tea, then grimaced. "How much sugar did I put in here?"

"Three."

"Three? I swear to god, I don't know where my head is these days." She plopped the cup down. "When I said I didn't have a brother, they looked at me like I'd grown horns. Then they buzzed around me, took me into an empty room and told me sit to down, that they'd look into it." Myers snorted. "Silly me. I thought they were serious. What they were actually doing was hitting the panic button. The next thing I knew, the director had arrived, with a posse of attorneys and security in tow. They treated me like I was a threat to national security."

Casey scribbled down *brother, imposter*, then said, "What did they do when you told them you don't have a brother?"

"They got all hoity-toity. The man had a power of attorney. His name was Steve Rose, so he had the same surname as Mom. How were they supposed to know he wasn't my mother's son? I'll tell them how. Where'd he been for the past month? I visited Mom every single day, except Sundays." She waved her plastic spoon at Casey. "Even God had a day of rest."

Something tugged at Casey. "Wait a minute. Why did the nurses say you must have forgotten?"

"They claimed that they called me when brother dearest showed up. I was away at a spa that weekend. The only time I didn't have my phone with me was when I was in the sauna. Do you think I'd risk missing a call telling me that Mom had snapped out of it? There were no messages on my phone. None. Nada." Her lips trembled. "How was I to know that the one weekend I'd be away, somebody claiming to be my brother would kidnap my mother?" She stared at Casey with bewildered eyes.

"I thought you said you visited her every day except Sundays."

"You have an ear for detail." Myers' brow crinkled. "That's a good trait for an investigator to have. Okay, I slacked off for one weekend, only because I won the spa stay." She shrugged and drank more tea, even though it made her grimace again. "I can't remember from what contest. Probably some form I filled in at a store."

Casey added the information to her notes.

"According to the nurses on duty that Saturday, my brother," Myers rolled her eyes, "wasn't in any hurry. He presented the paperwork, called the long-term care home, told the nurses that an ambulance would arrive in about an hour to transfer her, then went in and sat with her until it arrived. Can you believe that?" Myers shook her head. "Because he sounded nice and wasn't in a hurry to wheel her away, I guess they weren't suspicious."

"I gather she's not in the long-term care home."

"No. Once I got the name, I drove out there. They'd never heard of her, and they wouldn't let me look around the place to see if I could find her. Said they couldn't have me blundering into private rooms. It was posh," Myers added. "Way out of my budget. Even if I'd wanted Mom in there, I couldn't have afforded it."

"Did the police search the place for her?" Casey asked, assuming that Myers had contacted the authorities.

Myers bobbed her head. "Gave them a recent photo. Couldn't find her, on the grounds or in the files. Searched the admissions records of every damn long-term care facility in the country. Nothing. She was gone." Myers snapped her fingers. "Just like that. Oh, they say they're still working on the case, but I get the feeling they think it's a family dispute, especially since the signature and handwriting on the power of attorney matched my mother's."

"They did?"

"Yes. That's about the only thing those numbskull nurses did right. They made a copy."

"But the police must have confirmed you don't have a brother."

"Sure they did, but the nurses must have misheard, you know, because he only said it once. It's not indicated on the power of attorney itself." Myers' mouth pinched. "I guess I can't blame them for believing him."

"I don't suppose you have a copy of it?"

Myers sat back, eyes wide in mock disbelief. "Are you kidding? They behaved as if I was the criminal, and god forbid they give me anything that might work against them in a court case. All I care about is finding my mother. Once we've found her, then I'll think about suing."

Damn. Casey might not have gleaned anything useful from the document, but it was the only tangible item connected to the impostor.

"You could try asking Detective Walker if she'll make a copy for you. She's the most sympathetic cop out of the entire bunch. When I said I was going to hire an investigator, she's the only one who didn't tell me not to bother—but maybe she was relieved that I'd be somebody else's problem." Myers plopped her purse onto her lap and lifted out her wallet. "She might be willing to offer other information, too. Or she might tell you to take a hike. Here. Keep it. I have another one."

Casey took the business card from Myers. *Detective A. Walker. Missing Persons.* Feeling a mixture of fear and excitement, she glanced at the phone number, then tucked the card into the back of her notebook. "If the police know," her eyes went to her notes again, "that Steve Rose isn't your brother and you don't know him, why would they think it might be a family dispute?"

Myers waved a dismissive hand. "He could be a boyfriend." She chuckled at the question in Casey's eyes. "Mom's, not mine. I told you, they act like I'm the bad one. Maybe they think I hate him and so I claimed not to know who he is."

"How did your mother end up in a coma?"

"Well, there's another mystery for you." Myers leaned over the table. "Mom was at a work party, celebrating some project or other."

"What does she do?"

"She's a scientist. Anyway, she calls me around seven, tells me she's having a bad reaction to something in the buffet and the first aid person thinks she should go to emergency. Can I meet her there? Sure, I say. It didn't sound serious. She was joking with me on the phone. But by the time I got there, she was in a coma. Doctors couldn't explain it. Idiopathic. That's all they kept saying. Idiopathic. Which is a big word for 'We don't know why.'"

"There hadn't been any change in her condition over the month she was in hospital?"

"Nope. No improvement. No decline."

"Would it be possible for me to look around your mother's home, to get a sense of who she was—is?" *Shit.*

Fortunately Myers didn't notice Casey's slip. "Sure. The police didn't find anything useful, but another pair of eyes couldn't hurt. Do you want to go there now? You can follow me."

"Uh, I'm on a bike. The pedalling kind, not the vroom-vroom kind."

"Oh. How about I drive you and bring you back here when we're done?"

"That would be great. Thank you."

"Just let me finish my tea." Myers took another sip and made a face. "God, that's wretched. I don't know why I'm torturing myself. Or maybe I do."

Casey quickly read over her notes. Right now, she didn't have any more questions, which left the one topic that had nagged at her since Myers had called. She cleared her throat. "About my fee . . ."

Myers nodded and pulled a chequebook and pen from her purse. "Diane said something about a five thousand dollar retainer."

Casey grabbed her coffee cup and gulped down what was left. Five thousand? Holy shit. When she'd been in business for a while and had a track record, maybe. She set the cup down and wiped her mouth with the back of her hand. "Uh, Diane was joking. I charge fifty dollars an hour. I figure it'll take me a few days to do my preliminary investigation. So why don't you pay me for eighteen hours and then we'll meet and decide where to go from there."

"Eighteen hours. So that's . . ."

"Nine hundred dollars," Casey said, having already worked out the amount.

"Sounds good to me. Better than five thousand." Myers chuckled.

Casey shoved her notebook into her back pocket and watched Myers write the cheque. Why hadn't Diane mentioned her friend with the missing comatose mother when Casey had met her for dinner last week? You'd figure it would have come up in conversation at some point. "Do you know Diane well?"

"I went to high school with her mother." Myers ripped the cheque from the book and handed it to Casey. "We—her mother and I—have bumped into each other a few times over the years since then. When I ran into her yesterday, Diane was with her. I told them all about Mom, and that's when Diane suggested I contact you."

Myers was probably spilling the details about her mother to anyone who'd listen. Casey couldn't blame her. She'd be going crazy, too. "I'll thank her next time I see her." After examining the cheque, she folded it and slipped it into her front pocket. "Thank you, Ms. Myers."

Myers snorted. "Call me Ellen. I have enough on my mind without feeling old. At least you didn't call me ma'am."

"Sorry. Ellen."

"Much better. Shall we?" Ellen pushed back her chair.

Feeling on top of the world, Casey threw her coffee cup into the garbage and followed Ellen to her car. She was working her first case! The private investigators licence in her wallet meant something. Casey Cook, PI. Yes!

Chapter Two

CASEY STOOD IN the entrance hall and mentally ticked off what she hoped to accomplish in Jacqueline Rose's home: look for evidence of a son, though the police would have done the same; search for any indication that Mrs. Rose had a food allergy or health problem that Ellen wasn't aware of; learn more about Mrs. Rose in general, so she could identify red flags when questioning those who knew her.

A couple of toys lying in the hallway suggested at least one cat. "Who's taking care of the cat?"

"Marge, one of Mom's neighbours." Ellen's face scrunched up. "Poor things. They must be lonely."

"How many cats does your mother have?"

"Two. Max and Miles. I've been coming here for years, but they always hide when I'm around. According to Marge, when she comes over, they're usually under the bed in the guest room."

Casey grunted. "I think I'll start upstairs." She inwardly groaned when Ellen trailed after her. "I might have to open a few drawers. I'll make sure I put everything back in its place."

"Go ahead," Ellen said. "I want you to do whatever it takes to find my mother."

Casey paused on the landing until she located the bathroom. She opened the medicine cabinet. Nothing interesting. "Was your mother on any medication?"

"Not that I know of," Ellen said from the doorway. "Vitamins, maybe. She was still as fit as a fiddle. Could have retired a couple of years ago, but wanted to keep working."

"Is there an ensuite?"

"Not in these old houses."

Casey wandered back into the hallway and went into what appeared to be Mrs. Rose's home office. She sat down at the desk and turned on the computer. The police would have checked it, and Casey wasn't a computer wiz. She knew how to see hidden files and if any were encrypted, but that was it. She scanned Rose's Inbox. One hundred and eight messages. Might as well start at the top.

As soon as Casey opened the first email, Ellen cleared her throat. "Are you going to read *all* of them? I doubt you'll find anything interesting. The police didn't. No mention of a Steve Rose, or a brother I don't know about."

"They might have missed something."

Silence, then, "Look, I trust you. Do you mind if I go downstairs and watch some TV? Do you want something to eat? I'm starved. I might order a pizza."

Casey twisted around. "Sure," she said, trying not to sound elated.

"Great. Shout if you need anything." Ellen sauntered from the room.

When she heard the TV come on, Casey breathed a sigh of relief. She wasn't intending to steal the towels, but she didn't need Ellen breathing down her neck. Twenty minutes later, she browsed the computer's hard drive. Nothing jumped out at her. Apart from learning that Mrs. Rose had hundreds of cat photos, Casey found the computer a dead end. So was the guest room, but she spent an enjoyable five minutes cooing at the cats hiding underneath the bed.

In the master bedroom, Casey slid open the nightstand's drawer. A notepad, several pens, a half-empty pack of gum, a nail file . . . A grocery list was scribbled on the notepad's top page. Casey flipped through the rest of the pages. Empty. She dropped to her hands and knees and peered under the bed. Nothing but dust bunnies—wait. Something glinted on the hardwood floor. She pulled out the piece of tape and examined it. What looked like the corner of an envelope was stuck to one end. Assuming the envelope had been taped to something in this room, and close by . . .

Casey stood and eyed the nightstand. This time she emptied the drawer, but found nothing. She slid her hand behind the nightstand; her fingers hit something sticky. Her heart racing with excitement, she pulled the nightstand away from the wall. Aha!

Several pieces of tape were attached to the nightstand's back, suggesting the shape of a rectangle. The envelope they'd held in place was gone. Did it have anything to do with Mrs. Rose's disappearance, or had it contained items such as ID or money, and she'd hidden it there to conceal it from thieves? Was it taken before Mrs. Rose fell ill at the party, or later?

After making a note of the missing envelope and moving the nightstand back into its original position, Casey moved on to the bathroom and searched it more thoroughly. She found nothing of interest. Apparently Mrs. Rose hadn't hidden a medical condition from her daughter. It was time to look around the main floor.

Casey was descending the stairs when the doorbell rang.

"Good timing!" Ellen slapped a pizza box onto the coffee table and flipped open the lid. "Grab a drink from the fridge," she said as she lifted out a piece of pepperoni pizza and took a bite. "Oh, and bring a couple of plates, too."

Eager to ask Ellen the questions the upstairs search had raised, Casey did as she was told. "Apart from you and the cat-minder, has anyone else been in the house?"

"No."

"Are you sure?"

"Positive."

"Maybe your mother gave a key to someone you don't know about."

Ellen frowned. "Well, I suppose it's possible, but nothing's missing or out of place, as far as I know."

That naturally led to another question on Casey's mind. "Do you have your mother's personal items?"

Ellen's brow furrowed.

"Her purse. Any other items she might have had on her when she was taken to the hospital."

"Oh!" Ellen sipped her wine. Casey eyed the half-empty bottle, which Ellen apparently wanted all to herself. "I have her purse. Sissy brought it to the hospital. One of Mom's co-workers," she clarified in response to Casey's raised eyebrows.

"Was Sissy at the party?"

Ellen nodded. "She went to the hospital with Mom."

"Can I talk to her?"

"I'm sure she wouldn't mind." Ellen slid another piece of pizza onto her plate. "She and Mom have worked together for years. They were friendly outside work, too."

Casey grunted and bit into her second piece.

"I'll call her, tell her you want to see her."

"Thanks," Casey said around a mouthful of pizza. She swallowed. "Something might have been taped behind the nightstand in your mother's bedroom."

"Really," Ellen breathed.

"You don't know what it was?"

"I didn't even know anything was there. In the bedroom, you say." Ellen chugged more wine.

"What exactly did your mother do at work?"

"Something to do with cat food. She wasn't allowed to tell me any more than that, and if she'd tried, my eyes would have glazed over. Science isn't my forte." Ellen drank the rest of her wine and filled the glass again. "Whatever she did, she enjoyed it." Her eyes misted up. "Enjoys it. Enjoys it, damn it! Why did this have to happen to Mom? Why?" she wailed, then downed the wine in her glass in one go. After pushing her pizza aside, she poured a refill.

Oh, boy. Casey put down her pizza. She'd better ask her remaining questions while Ellen could still provide coherent answers. "The neighbour that's taking care of the cats, she lives . . ."

"Next door. House with the blue door and silly garden gnome."

"Do you mind if I look through your mother's purse?"

"No. But it's not here. It's at home. We can drop in there on the way back to the coffee shop."

What? "You know what? I've already imposed enough. I can take the bus back. And you might want to crash here tonight. You're already here—"

"You don't think I should drive, do you."

Casey opened her mouth to protest, but Ellen held up her hand. "You're right. And frankly, I want to finish this bottle and go to bed. Why don't you call me about the purse tomorrow and we'll arrange a time?"

"Sure." She'd noted down Ellen's number when they were at the coffee shop.

"Finish your pizza before you run off."

Casey made fast work of her slice, then took a quick look around the main floor and basement. Apart from the address book she found next to the phone in the kitchen, which didn't list anyone with the last name Rose, nothing caught her eye.

"Thanks for dinner. I'll be in touch tomorrow," Casey said from the living room archway.

Lounging on the sofa, Ellen nodded and lifted her wine glass.

CASEY FUMBLED AROUND in her pocket for correct change and inserted it into the bus's fare box. She stumbled down the aisle as the bus lurched forward, and slid into an empty seat. Staring out the window, she reviewed her conversation with Mrs. Rose's neighbour. She hadn't been much help. No sign of anyone ever being in the house, other than Ellen. No strange mail, which Casey knew was true because she'd sorted through the pile herself. The neighbour didn't listen to phone messages, but Ellen did, and hadn't heard any weird ones.

This detective work was more mundane than she'd expected, but at least she had a case. An actual case! Which reminded her . . . She pulled out her phone and called Diane. "I'm calling to thank you for recommending me to Ellen Myers," she said after they'd exchanged the usual greetings.

"She called you?" Diane shrieked. "No need to thank me. I mentioned you to shut her up."

"What do you mean?"

"When you ask someone, 'How are you?' you just want them to say, 'Fine,' right? Especially when they're someone you run into maybe once every five years. But, oh my god, she started blubbering and telling us about her mother, and how stressed she is."

"Come on, Diane, her mother's missing."

"I know, but we were on our way to meet my father for dinner, okay? Anyway, I said that if the cops were doing diddly-squat, she should hire a private investigator, and, hey, my friend happens to be one."

"Well, thanks." So Diane didn't really believe she could find Mrs. Rose. Big deal.

"Oh, while I have you, I ran into Leah earlier today. She dropped a lot of hints about you."

Casey's heart pounded. "Hints? What kind of hints?"

"Oh, that she might be interested in seeing you . . . alone."

Leah? Really? "I might be interested in seeing her."

Diane burst into laughter. "Give me a break. You don't have to be a PI to figure out that you're hot for her. Do you want me to give her your phone number?"

Was the sky blue? The pope Catholic? "Sure."

Another chortle. "Don't try playing it cool with her. You'll make yourself look like an ass. Anyway, gotta go. Talk to you soon."

"Yeah, bye." Casey hung up and slipped the phone into her pocket. Okay, no need to get excited. Diane had probably misinterpreted things. Leah would wonder why the hell Diane was giving her Casey's phone number. After all, Leah was one of the cool gals, one of those women who strolled into a room and effortlessly turned everyone to putty. She was cute, warm, intelligent—well, Casey assumed those last two. She'd hardly exchanged more than two words with her, but Leah was always smiling, always poised, always surrounded by women hanging on her every word. Diane must have gotten it wrong, but it was nice to imagine it was true for a second.

Casey gazed out the window until her phone rang. She didn't recognize the number but answered anyway. "Hello."

"Hi, Casey, it's Leah."

Leah? *The* Leah? Casey straightened in her seat. "Uh, hi."

"Diane just gave me your phone number. She said you're interested in getting together."

What?

"I think it's a cool idea, so I figured I'd call while the iron is hot."

Leah thinks it's cool? Casey cleared her throat. "Um, yeah, I—"

"Are you busy tomorrow night?"

"Uh, no, I'm—"

"Do you want to meet for a pizza and then see a movie or something?"

"Sure. How about—"

"There's a restaurant on Queen that makes delicious pizza. You want to go there?"

"Sure."

"It's a bit upscale," Leah said. "No jeans."

"Okay. I'll—"

"I'll text you the address. Want to meet at 6:00?"

"Okay."

"Great. See you tomorrow." The line went dead.

Casey stared at her phone. Had that actually happened, or had she dozed off and dreamed the conversation? A text from Leah arrived. Nope, no dream. She read the address, then pocketed her phone. Tomorrow would be an interesting day in more ways than one.

CASEY SLID INTO the booth at the greasy spoon, plunked her bike helmet on the seat next to her, and stuck out her hand. "Casey Cook."

Detective Walker wiped her fingers on a napkin and reached across the table to shake Casey's hand. "Walker."

"Thanks for agreeing to see me."

Walker shrugged. "No problem."

"Are you still—"

A harried waitress stopped at their table and pulled out an order pad. "What do you want?"

Casey scratched her head. "A coffee, please." The waitress scribbled on her pad and moved on to another table.

"Are you still working the Rose case?" Casey asked.

"Of course we are—officially. It's on the books. Realistically, we've hit a dead end. We can't do much more until a tip comes in, and it's not as if it's the only case we have." Walker chewed on a fry. "Listen, I won't discourage you from looking into Jacqueline Rose's disappearance, but you'd better not be taking Myers for a ride."

"I'm not! I'm going to see what I can dig up, and if that turns out to be nothing, I'll tell her."

Walker studied her. "You look a little young to be a PI."

"I'm twenty-three." Casey reached into her back pocket. "Do you want to see my licence?"

Walker's mouth twitched. "It won't have your birthdate."

"Right."

"Driver's licence?"

"I don't have one."

"Give me your PI licence then, so I can confirm your name."

Casey handed it over and sat on tenterhooks while Walker examined the card. "It looks legit," Walker said, handing it back. "So, PI Cook, what can I do for you?"

"Ms. Myers said you checked the handwriting on the power of attorney the bogus son gave you."

"Yep. According to our analysis, there's a 91.5 percent chance that the handwriting is Jacqueline Rose's, and it's a duly filled out and signed power of attorney. I can understand why the hospital administration accepted it."

Not one hundred percent, then. Casey would keep an open mind. "What about the witnesses?"

"The attorney passed away two years ago. One of his assistants was the other witness. We faxed her the document and she confirmed that it's her signature. Since it was fifteen years ago and she's witnessed thousands of documents, she couldn't remember signing Rose's power of attorney, but she said she can't remember the ones she signed last year, either."

"Do you have any idea who Steve Rose is?"

Walker shook her head.

"What about hospital cameras? Do you know what he looks like?"

Walker squirted more ketchup on her fries and stuck another one in her mouth. The waitress returned and, after plunking a coffee down in front of Casey, refilled Walker's cup. "We have a grainy image," Walker said when she'd finished chewing.

"Can I get a copy?" Casey said excitedly.

"No."

Casey blew out an exasperated sigh. "Why not? How am I supposed to find him if I can't show his picture to anyone?"

"We didn't just take Ms. Myers' missing persons report and file it. We looked into it, questioned a lot of people, in both Mrs. Rose's personal and professional lives. They all saw the picture. Nobody recognized him."

"Maybe I'll find someone you didn't interview," Casey said.

Walker pointed a fry at her. "I'll tell you what. If, during the course of your, um, investigation, you find someone we didn't talk to, call me, and *I'll* show them the photo."

"But—"

"Don't worry, I won't steal your thunder." Walker sipped her coffee. "Rose, or whatever his name is, showed the nurses ID with a local address. Unfortunately they didn't make a copy of it, but we followed up on every Steve Rose in the city. Nothing."

So whoever he was, he'd used a convincing fake ID. "What about fingerprints?"

"We didn't find any we couldn't account for."

"He must have touched something."

"Sure, but that doesn't mean he left behind decent fingerprints." Walker smiled wryly. "We've gone above and beyond on this one, considering we're not even sure a crime was committed. After all, the guy had a legit power of attorney."

"But—"

"My gut says something isn't right. The daughter's never heard of the guy. Huge red flag right there. It's why I—we haven't closed the case."

Now Casey understood why the case wasn't a high priority. Everyone except Walker believed it should be closed. "What do you think has happened to her?" she asked. Walker must have formed a theory.

"I honestly don't know. Why would someone kidnap a woman in a coma, and what would he do with her? She wasn't on a ventilator, but she has to be fed, turned, checked. And where could she be? We've checked every medical facility in the country." Walker coughed into her napkin. "What have you discovered?"

Casey hesitated. "Uh . . ."

Walker rolled her eyes. "Do you mind if I give you a little advice?"

"No. Anything you can share with me would be great." Casey clasped her hands on the table and stared in anticipation at Walker, who grinned.

"Listen, I like your attitude. I have a good feeling about you. If you're going to get anywhere, you'll need cops on your side, okay? You share with me, I share with you. And sometimes you'll want someone with a gun and handcuffs around. Trust me on that. So I'll ask you again. What have you discovered?"

"Not much," Casey admitted. "I've only just started working on the case." She recounted the important parts of her meeting with Ellen and her search of Mrs. Rose's house.

"Good catch about the nightstand," Walker said. Casey squirmed when blood rushed to her cheeks, then her shoulders slumped when Walker added, "Useless without knowing what was in the envelope, though."

"Do you think you'll—we'll find her?"

Walker pushed her plate away. "I don't know. We have her information out there. I suppose we could put up posters, but what would we say? If you see a woman being wheeled down the street on a gurney, call us? Wherever she is, she's inside, where nobody except her supposed son will ever see her."

But what would anyone want with a comatose woman? "Do you think she's still alive?"

"I don't know." The possibility that she wasn't hung between them. "Listen, if you want to bounce something off me about the case, call me, okay? You might tell me something that connects a couple of dots."

"I'll do that." Knowing she could consult with Walker instantly made her first case less intimidating.

"I'll call you if I need to ask you something." Walker wagged her finger. "Or if we receive complaints about a nosy PI."

"You won't!"

"Can I have your card?"

Her card? Shit. She hadn't thought about business cards, but gamely patted her pockets. "Uh . . ."

Walker shook her head and pulled a business card and pen from her blazer pocket. "Here, write your number on the back. Give me your email address, too."

Feeling like an ass, Casey did so.

Walker took the card and stared at it. "Casey Cook. That's it? No snappy company name?" Casey opened her mouth to reply, then clamped it shut when Walker winked. "I bet this is your first case."

"Uh, yeah." It wouldn't take a crack detective to figure that out. If her absolutely stunning display of confidence hadn't tipped Walker off, the date on her licence would have.

Walker snorted. "And it's to find a missing comatose woman. Jesus. The guys back at the station won't believe this."

"Do you think you can keep it between us?"

"I suppose I can." Walker bit her lip. "For now. Anyway, I have to run." She waggled her eyebrows. "Thanks for lunch."

Casey bit back a surprised retort. "Yeah. Sure."

Walker slid from the booth and patted Casey's shoulder as she passed her. "We're going to get along just fine."

There went more of Ellen's retainer than Casey had expected. She looked over her shoulder and watched Walker stroll from the diner. The waitress slapped the bill onto the table. "Here you go. Pay at the cash," she muttered.

Casey read the amount and sighed. After leaving the tip—fifteen percent, despite the waitress's attitude—she settled the bill at the cash.

Outside, she sat on her bike with her helmet resting on her knee, mentally reviewing her to do list. "Make sure you wear your helmet," a familiar voice yelled. Walker, stopped at the traffic light, rolled up her window. If Walker hadn't already made Casey feel like a five-year-old, she would have succeeded now. Casey waved, but Walker pulled away without a backward glance. Well, it wasn't as if Casey had expected any respect as a PI . . .

She refocused on her mental list. She'd called Ellen and arranged to kill two birds with one stone: rummage through Mrs. Rose's purse and meet with Sissy, but not until tomorrow night. Her date with Leah came first. Butterflies took flight in Casey's stomach. *Focus, focus!* She'd go home and, uh, brainstorm, while she counted down the hours to her date. *Uh-huh,* she thought, admitting that she'd be useless for the rest of the afternoon. She'd put in extra hours tomorrow. She'd promised Ellen eighteen hours, and Ellen would get them.

Chapter Three

Casey stepped off the bus and darted into the bus shelter to avoid getting wet. Did it have to rain? Her fantasy of breezing into the restaurant and sweeping Leah off her feet hadn't included wet hair and the damp bedraggled look. She glanced at her watch. Since she didn't want to be late, she'd arrived twenty minutes early and could afford to wait out the shower, while appealing to every god and goddess she'd heard of to give the sun a turn. One of them must have taken pity on her. With five minutes to go, the rain eased up. Casey seized the opportunity to jog into the restaurant.

The greeter smiled at her. "Table for . . . ?"

"I'm meeting someone. Maybe she's here? Leah . . ."

The greeter glanced at the table plan in front of her. "Leah who?"

Leah . . . she didn't know. Leah had always been "Leah, the popular and self-assured woman who would never look at Casey twice."

The greeter tapped her pencil against the table plan.

"Do you mind if I pop into the restaurant and see if she's here?"

"No, go right ahead."

Casey wandered past the reception podium and scanned the dining room. Shit, Leah wasn't here. She checked her watch again. Three minutes to go. "I'll just wait here," she said, trying not to look as if she was worried about being stood up. She wasn't worried. Nope. Not worried.

Ten minutes later, it was becoming more difficult to smile at the greeter every time their eyes met. "What time were you supposed to be meeting your friend?" the woman asked.

"Six."

The greeter glanced at her watch and frowned.

"She's always late," Casey said with an exaggerated sigh.

"Why don't I seat you? I'm sure she'll be here soon."

"Sure." It would be better than being stared at, but what if Leah didn't show up?

The greeter led her to a window table. "Here you go." She set two menus on the table.

Casey sat down and stared out the window. If it was anyone else, she wouldn't think twice about pulling out her phone to call and ask where the hell she was. But in this case, Casey had to play it cool, not sound desperate. She clenched her hands on her lap and resisted the urge to look at her watch again. What if Leah didn't show? Should she slink out and hope the greeter had gone to the bathroom, or order dinner and pretend that she hadn't just experienced a humiliating rejection every time someone looked over at the poor woman sitting by herself?

A waiter stopped at the table to fill the water glasses. Was that sympathy in his eyes? The evening hadn't even started and it was already a nightmare. Casey struggled to suppress her rising panic. Leah wouldn't set up a date and then blow her off, right? Maybe anxiety made Leah lose track of time. She was probably as nervous as Casey.

A gleaming red sports car pulled into a parking spot outside Casey's window. The driver's door opened and Leah stepped out, looking as if she'd spent the afternoon being pampered at a spa. Okay, so maybe she wasn't anxious. At least she was here! Casey's throat tightened. She grabbed her water glass and gulped half its contents, then set it on the table and smiled when Leah approached.

"Hey." Leah pulled out the chair across from Casey and smiled.

"Hi."

They stared at each other.

"Have you been here before?" Leah asked.

"No," Casey said while her mind screamed, *Where the hell were you? It's almost 6:15!* Her fingernails dug into her palms.

"Have you ordered?"

"No."

They both reached for their menus. Casey scanned the offerings. Typical Italian fare. Normally she'd go for lasagna or tortellini, but

Leah had mentioned pizza on the phone. "What do you like on your pizza?" she asked, her nose still buried in the menu.

"Meat. Pepperoni, ham, beef, bacon."

Hmm, it sounded like the meat-lovers pizza was right up Leah's alley.

"With cheese. Lots and lots of cheese."

Casey preferred a pizza lighter on meat and cheese, but the meat-lovers pizza wouldn't kill her. She closed her menu and swallowed. "You look nice."

Leah flicked back her hair. "Thanks."

The waiter arrived and turned to Leah. "What can I get you to drink?"

"White wine."

"Certainly. And for you?"

"Coke," Casey said.

He made a note and eyed the closed menus. "Are you ready to order?"

"Sure," Casey said, since the waiter was still focused on her. "Do you think a medium pizza will be big enough?" she asked Leah.

"Um, yeah."

"Okay. One medium meat-lovers pizza, with extra cheese."

The waiter nodded. "Is that all?"

"No," Leah said, at the same time Casey nodded. "I'll have the fettuccine."

What? She'd thought . . . she couldn't eat a medium pizza by herself.

The waiter turned back to Casey. "Are you sure you want a medium?"

No! "Yes." And if he could run along before embarrassing her any further, that would be great.

"All right. One medium meat-lovers pizza with Coke, and one fettuccine with a white wine." He gathered up the menus and left.

Casey and Leah stared at each other. "How have you been? How's your day been?" Casey asked.

Leah launched into a detailed account of her day from the moment she'd risen: the TV shows she'd watched, the stores she'd visited, the food she'd eaten—and that only took them to mid-afternoon. Apart from "uh-huh" and "cool," Casey couldn't get a word in edgewise. Leah paused when the waiter returned with their drinks, then picked up mid-sentence and talked until their meals were on the table. Her brows shot up. "You have quite the appetite."

"I thought maybe you'd have some," Casey said hopefully. "You did say on the phone that this place has great pizza." She couldn't keep the irritation out of her voice, but Leah didn't notice.

"It does, but I wasn't in the mood for pizza tonight."

Something Casey would have appreciated knowing before she'd ordered a pizza three times larger than she could eat. Okay, she hadn't asked Leah if she wanted pizza; she'd assumed. But did Leah honestly think she was ordering a medium for herself? She could have spoken up, if she was aware of Casey's existence. So far, Casey felt invisible. Maybe Leah was nervous. Some people clammed up, others couldn't shut up. Normally Casey's nerves would make her stumble over her words, but her ruffled feathers were overruling the butterflies—when she had the chance to open her mouth. Well, it was still early. Maybe Leah would calm down and notice that she wasn't eating alone.

Casey lifted a slice of pizza onto her plate and flashed back to Ellen knocking back her wine. Pizza for dinner twice in a row. Good thing she loved it. Leah popped a forkful of fettuccine into her mouth . . . and stopped talking. Casey quickly finished chewing her mouthful of pizza. "I'm working a case," she blurted.

"A case? Oh, right, Diane mentioned that you're trying the PI thing."

Trying the PI thing? She hadn't sweated over getting her licence on a whim.

"What's the case about?"

Casey wanted to kick herself. She didn't want a reputation for blabbing her clients' private business to anyone who'd listen. "A missing person case. I can't talk about the details, though. Confidential." Why had she even brought it up? "What do you do?" she asked, realizing that she didn't know.

"I'm working on my thesis for my PhD in psychology."

"What's your thesis about?"

"The details would bore you. Let's just say it concerns relationships." Leah's eyes lit up. "Guess what I did last weekend? Went to that new club on Beach Street. Have you been?"

Casey shook her head.

"You pretty much have to know someone to get in."

Maybe they could go after supper, not that Casey was big on clubbing. She'd prefer a movie followed by a coffee, and then home to bed. She wasn't the "arrive at eleven and stay up until four" type.

"Let's see, who was there." Leah pursed her lips, then reeled off a list of names and proceeded to gossip about people Casey didn't know or care about. She could feel her eyes glazing over, and only Leah's every third or fourth word got through. This date was a disaster. Mismatched didn't begin to describe it. And maybe she was being sensitive, but she'd bet Leah told everyone else the details of her thesis. Why had Leah wanted to get together with a dumb PI? How could Casey politely wiggle her way out of the movie so she could cut her losses, go home, and marvel at how some people were best admired from afar?

When Casey had finished her third—and final—piece of pizza, Leah finally lapsed into silence. The waiter came over to see how they were doing. He lifted Leah's empty plate from the table, then frowned at the half of the pizza still waiting to be eaten. "Was it all right?"

"It was fine," Casey said, aghast.

"You sure?"

"Yes." Jesus, she hated waiters who called attention to how much she had or hadn't eaten. They were supposed to make the dining experience a pleasurable one, not embarrass people.

"I can put this into a takeout container for you."

"Sure, do that." Anything to get rid of the guy.

He whisked the pizza off the table and strode away. Casey and Leah stared at each other. The seconds dragged by. Leah swallowed the last of her wine and narrowed her eyes at Casey. "Maybe we should skip the movie."

Casey instantly relaxed. "Good idea. I'm glad we met for dinner, but—"

"Let's go back to your place."

"What?"

"We can't go to mine. My roommate's home."

"What are you talking about?"

Leah snorted. "Do I have to draw you a diagram? Come on! So we're not exactly hitting it off. I'm not looking for anything serious, anyway." She leaned forward. "Sometimes it's better with someone you don't click with on a conversational level. No talking. Just raw action."

Wait, wait, wait! Leah wasn't suggesting . . . "Look—I mean—we just met."

"We've been passing each other at parties for years."

"I pass a lot of people at parties. That doesn't mean . . . I like to know someone a little better before I take that step, okay?"

"You're so cute," Leah said with a giggle. "I'm liking this idea more and more. What do you need to know?"

Her last name, for a start—hopefully very early on in their relationship, you know, the one they'd have before they slept together. "Leah . . . it's not you, okay. I don't sleep with people I hardly know."

Leah drew back. She arched a skeptical brow. "Is it that we can't go back to your place for some reason? You're not one of those sad cases who still lives with her parents, are you?"

"Well, I live with my grandmother, but—"

"Is she senile?"

"No!" She needed Gran more than Gran needed her.

"Okay, so your place is out." Leah blew a stray hair out of her face. "There's my car."

"Leah, the answer is no."

Leah shrugged. "Fine. I already have plenty of people on my list for when I'm feeling raunchy. I'm always looking to add more, though." She reached across the table and ran her finger down Casey's forearm. "Last chance."

Casey jerked her arm away. So this was what their "date" was about? She was auditioning for a spot on Leah's booty call list? God, what a waste of time! Did Diane know about this?

Leah scowled and pushed back her chair. "Thanks for dinner."

"But . . ." As she watched Leah sashay away, she wanted to shout, "Come back and pay your half of the bill," but pride wouldn't let her.

The waiter returned with her takeout container. His eyes flicked to Leah's empty place. "Coffee?"

"Just the bill, please," she muttered. Mercifully, it only took him a minute to present the bill on a tray—with one candy. Casey frowned at the total. At this rate, she'd have nothing left. She fished several bills from her wallet—enough to cover the total plus a fifteen percent tip—and skulked from the restaurant carrying her leftover pizza. She glimpsed Leah sitting in the front seat of her car, gabbing on her phone. Probably going down her list.

Casey was almost at the bus shelter when a tidal wave instantly drenched her. The red sports car continued on past the deep puddle near the curb, zooming into the distance. Casey stared after it, then pulled out her phone and dialed Diane's number. "Call me, okay?" she said through gritted teeth when she got voice mail. Maybe it was for the best that Diane hadn't answered.

When the bus arrived, she climbed aboard and ignored the curious looks from those who wondered why only half of her was soaked. As soon as she sat down, she realized that she'd left the pizza in the bus shelter. No great loss. Let someone eat it who needed it more than she did. Of course, a minute before her stop, the skies opened up again—and just when she was starting to feel pleasantly damp. Apparently her fervent pleas to the rain gods earlier that evening had expired.

She hopped off the bus and ducked into the coffee shop where she'd met Ellen. Now she'd have to buy a coffee or donut. Some people would hover in the doorway, making it clear that they were only there to shelter, but Casey was the type who ordered something because she'd needed to use a washroom. She mustered whatever dignity she could and squelched over to the counter.

Weird, nobody was there, but the shop was open, and a couple sat in conversation at one of the window tables.

"Hi."

Casey jumped. "Oh, hi," she said, to an apparently invisible person.

The owner's daughter rose from her crouch behind the counter. "Sorry, I didn't mean to frighten you."

"Where's your dad?" He usually worked the counter on weekday evenings.

"Out with my mom. It's their anniversary, so I'm filling in. I haven't seen you in here for a while."

"I was just here the other day, to meet—" She stopped. Why tell . . . shoot, what was the owner's daughter's name again? Emma? No, Emily! Why humiliate herself a second time by telling Emily that she was a PI? Emily was probably studying for her PhD in nuclear physics. "I guess I usually come in here when you're not working."

Come to think of it, Casey hadn't run into her for months. "You still working here, or just filling in for tonight?"

"I'm doing early mornings, before school."

Curiosity and politeness compelled Casey to ask, "What are you studying?"

"I'm doing a PhD in computer science."

Please, please, don't ask me what I do.

"What are you up to these days?" Emily asked.

Shit. "Nothing important," Casey mumbled. "I'll take a coffee to go, please," she said stiffly.

"Sure." Emily filled a paper coffee cup and pressed a cover onto it. She handed it to Casey and smiled. "You look nice." She paused. "Meeting someone special?"

Nope. Not meeting anyone special; hadn't met anyone special. And didn't Emily notice that half her outfit had shrunk? "No, I'm actually on my way home," Casey said, handing her a five dollar bill.

"You okay? You look a little down," Emily said as she rang up the coffee.

"I'm fine. I just got caught in the rain, that's all." Casey accepted her change and glanced out the window. "It looks like the rain is slowing down. I'd better—"

Emily lifted a finger. "Wait." She moved down the counter to the Danish and muffin area. "Take a Danish with you. On the house."

"No, it's okay."

"Take it. It's almost closing time, so it'll only go to waste."

"You sure?"

Emily nodded. "You like raspberry, right?"

"Uh, yeah," Casey said, surprised that Emily remembered.

Emily slid a raspberry Danish into a bag, then used the tongs to pick up another Danish.

"One's already more than generous," Casey quickly said.

"The other one's for your grandmother. She likes the strawberry ones." Emily rolled the bag shut. "There you go."

"Thank you."

They stared at each other. "Well, I should get going," Casey said. "Thanks again for the Danishes."

"No problem." When Casey pulled open the door, Emily called, "Casey!"

One hand holding the door, Casey twisted toward the counter.

"Good seeing you."

"Yeah, you too." She returned Emily's wave, then narrowly averted smashing her face into the door and stepped outside. Suddenly the world felt brighter, despite the gloomy sky and the light shower making the puddles dance. A little kindness could go a long way. Or was it pity? Either way, she appreciated Emily's gesture.

Not wanting to scare Gran, Casey shouted, "It's just me," when she got home. Her last words to Gran when leaving had been, "Don't wait up." Casey checked her watch—8:35. Woo-hoo!

To her surprise, the TV was off and the sofa empty. "Gran?"

Heels clicked along the hardwood in the hallway. Gran, all made up and in one of her church dresses, stopped in front of the mirror near the front door and examined herself.

"Gran." Casey walked over to her. "Gran!"

Gran jumped. "What are you shouting for? I have my hearing aids turned on."

"You weren't answering me."

"I'm busy!" Gran snapped open her purse, fished out a brush, and dragged it through her hair.

"Where are you going?"

"Marsha's rounding a bunch of us up to go to a movie." She dropped the brush back into the purse and turned to Casey. "I thought you were on a date."

"It didn't work out."

"How can you know it didn't work out?" Gran bellowed. "You were only gone for five minutes."

"Trust me, sometimes you can tell." She lifted the bag containing the Danishes. "From Emily at the coffee shop. One for me, one for you."

Gran peeked into the bag. "The strawberry's mine."

"Don't worry, I won't eat it."

"It's still early. Call one of your friends."

"Nah." With her luck, if she ventured outside again, she'd get hit by a bus.

"Don't worry, somewhere out there is a girl just for you."

"I'm not worried! I'm only twenty-three. It's not like when you were younger, when if you weren't married by the time you turned sixteen, there was something wrong with you."

Gran snorted. "It wasn't that bad. And don't knock marrying young. We didn't need all that in-vitro fertilizer back then, because we didn't wait until we were old before we tried to get pregnant." She wagged a finger. "And don't get me started on substitute mothers."

"Surrogate mothers," Casey said with a sigh.

"Next they'll be buying babies at the store, like out of a science fiction movie. Thank god I'll be dead by then. Though some things have changed for the better, eh?" She threw her arm around Casey and squeezed her. "Promise me you'll get married before I kick it. I bet the wedding will cost a fortune, with two brides."

"Two brides who won't need wedding dresses and a fancy wedding." At least, she wouldn't.

Gran shook her head. "First things first, though, eh? You'll find someone, don't worry." She pursed her lips. "You know, I've always wondered where they put it."

"Put what?"

"The fertilizer."

It took Casey a few seconds to understand what Gran was saying. "It's in vitro *fertilization*, Gran." She kept her voice even with difficulty. "They used to call them test tube babies, maybe because they did it in a test tube."

Gran's expression grew even more confused. "It must have been a big test tube. Anyway, I'd better get going, or they'll go without me." She reached for the front door handle.

"It's raining," Casey said, pulling an umbrella from the stand. She supposed she could have taken one with her to the restaurant, but she tended to forget umbrellas on the bus. Plus, it would have gotten in the way—as if that mattered now.

Gran took it from her and opened the door. Her eyes glinted mischievously. "Don't wait up." Casey could swear that Gran giggled as she pulled the door shut behind her.

Time to get on with her exciting evening. No point going online and seeing if anyone wanted to chat. All her friends would be out. After putting Gran's Danish into the fridge and scarfing down her own, Casey changed into her pyjamas. She'd just settled onto the sofa and flicked to a movie when a telltale honk told her the cat was barfing up a hairball.

Yep, it was that kind of night.

Chapter Four

Casey rode the elevator up to the Downtown General Hospital's sixth floor and squared her shoulders, trying to exude an air of confidence as she strolled up to the nurse's station.

A frazzled-looking nurse glanced up from a chart, then came over to the counter. "Can I help you?"

She read the nurse's name tag: Stephanie. "I'm here on behalf of the family of Jacqueline Rose," Casey said, using the voice that made her sound older on the phone. "I was wondering if I could ask you a few questions about the man who transferred Mrs. Rose to another facility."

"No."

"No?"

"No."

"I've already conferred with the lead detective on the case," Casey said, hoping that would give her some street cred with Stephanie.

Stephanie squinted at her. "Who did you say you were?"

"Casey Cook. Private investigator."

Stephanie snorted. "I know why you're here."

"You do?"

"By family, you mean Mrs. Myers, right?" When Casey didn't reply, Stephanie nodded and folded her arms. "You can tell Mrs. Myers that sniffing around here won't get her any money. I'm not saying a word."

"I'm not here because she's suing the hospital. She's trying to find her mother."

"Sure, she is," Stephanie drawled. "And I'm the Queen of England."

Casey huffed. "Look, I was just wondering if you knew what the man looked like."

"No, I don't."

"Is there someone on duty who was here the day Mrs. Rose went missing?"

Stephanie's face tightened. "Allegedly went missing."

"You don't think she's missing?"

"I think I have patients to attend to, and if you're really an investigator, you should have figured it all out by now. Mrs. Rose goes missing over the one weekend Mrs. Myers is away. Normally that woman would be here on Saturday. But not that weekend. And now she has you asking questions, hoping we'll give you something she can use against us." Stephanie tapped her temples. "Put it all together, Sherlock. Now, I suggest you leave, or I'll call security."

Casey decided not to find out if Stephanie was bluffing. Frustrated, she strode back to the elevator and rode it down to the ground floor. Could Stephanie be right? Why would Ellen arrange to kidnap her own mother, especially when Mrs. Rose was in a coma . . . or had that been a precipitating factor? Kidnapping a conscious person who didn't want to go along with a plan to bilk the hospital wouldn't work. Nah, Ellen had hired Casey to find her mother . . . but was that for show? Had she chosen Casey because she'd figured an inexperienced PI wouldn't solve the case? Or was that Casey's lack of confidence talking?

Should she have flashed her licence? Made up a better story for good old Stephanie? At least her brief encounter with Attila the Nurse had gleaned a new piece of information: PIs were below cockroaches on the respect totem pole.

With a sigh, she mounted her bike and pushed off, then braked. Wait a minute. Her conversation with Stephanie hadn't been a total loss. *Mrs. Rose goes missing over the one weekend Mrs. Myers is away.* She pulled her notebook from her pocket and read over her notes from her meeting with Ellen. *Won a spa weekend getaway.* Hmm. She shoved the notebook into her back pocket and slipped her phone from the front one.

Ellen picked up on the first ring. "Casey? Do you have news?"

Casey cringed at the hope in Ellen's voice. "No. I'm calling to ask you about that spa weekend you won. The one you went to on the weekend your mother disappeared."

"Oh, yeah."

"Can you tell me more about it? How did you arrange the weekend? Did you have a choice, or did you have to go on those specific dates? Are you sure you don't remember which contest it was?"

"Jeez, give me a minute to think." Silence, then, "I had to go that weekend." Ellen paused. "They called me, told me I'd won. We arranged everything right then, on the phone."

"Do you still have their number on your phone?"

"It was over five weeks ago."

She'd take that as a no. "Which contest was it?"

Ellen let out an exasperated sigh. "I don't remember. I enter everything—online, offline, radio and TV contests. You don't enter, you can't win. It's not the first thing I've won."

Great. "What was the name on the bill?"

"What bill? The desk told me everything was taken care of, that the booking instructions specifically said not to bother me with trivial details like the bill. It was all expenses paid. I didn't have to worry about a cent."

Casey wanted to scream. "Which spa was it?" Surely Ellen would know that.

"Radiant Rejuvenations. It's in Dunberg."

Shit, that was about an hour away. She'd have to figure out how to get there. Maybe take a bus or commuter train? Mistake number one: she hadn't asked Ellen to pay for expenses. Adding them to Ellen's final bill wouldn't be honest. Something to remember for her next case, assuming there was one.

"I had one weekend away. One weekend," Ellen wailed. "One lousy weekend after weeks of keeping vigil at Mom's bedside whenever I could."

"I realize that. I'm not—"

"I don't understand why the hospital says I answered the phone and told them it was okay to move Mom. I was in the sauna when they called. Then we had supper—"

"We?"

"Me and Trudy."

"You didn't mention that you took a friend."

"I didn't. We met in the lobby when I was checking in, and we hit it off. After supper, we, uh . . ."

They got wasted, or at least Ellen did. "This was on the day your mother disappeared?"

"Yes. Well, Trudy and I hung out together all weekend. You know, she said she'd email me, but she never did. I would have noticed, but when I came home and found out Mom was gone, everything else went out the window."

Casey waited while Ellen took a slurp from a drink. "Was Trudy in the sauna, too?"

"No. She said she wanted to lie down for a bit."

"Who suggested the sauna?"

"I don't know," Ellen shrieked. "Why do you care so much about the flipping spa? That's not going to find Mom."

"I'm wondering if the contest was bogus." And whether Trudy was a plant who'd answered Ellen's phone when the hospital had called.

"What do you mean?" Ellen breathed.

"I'm wondering if someone deliberately made sure you were out of town and away from your phone. Since you don't remember the contest or anything, I'll try to find out who paid for your stay, but the spa probably won't give me the information." She'd try anyway, and in person. It was easy to hang up on someone, not so easy to ignore someone making a fuss at Reception.

"They'll give it to me! I'll make up some story about my accountant needing a copy of the bill and the contest people won't give it to me, or the contest people claiming I owe them part of the bill, or something like that."

Casey's heart raced. "Don't call. Show up at the spa."

"When do you want to go?"

Sweet.

"We're meeting Sissy tonight," Ellen said. "How about tomorrow?"

"Sure."

"Sissy's looking forward to meeting the investigator I've hired."

Casey wasn't sure whether to be pleased or afraid. "Tell her I'll have lots of questions for her."

"Oh, I have a good feeling about the spa visit," Ellen squealed. "We're on the right track! See you later."

"Bye." Casey hung up, then made a note to ask Ellen for Trudy's full name.

SIPPING HER COFFEE, Casey listened to Sissy gossip about her co-workers. So far, she'd learned that Mrs. Rose worked in the cat food formulation department, that there'd recently been tension between Mrs. Rose and her boss, Mike Hargrave, and that pet food was a multi-billion dollar business and extremely competitive. Oh, and that the receptionist was carrying on a torrid affair with one of the scientists, that Jinny, another scientist, stole people's desserts from the fridge, that Phyllis, an administrative assistant, wouldn't use any of the dishes in the kitchen because she felt the scientists didn't adequately wash their hands, and that Henry, another scientist, had been caught eating a sample formulation—more than once! Casey had put down her half-eaten Danish during that part of the conversation.

"What about the party?" she said when Sissy finally stopped talking long enough for her to get a word in edgewise. "You were with Mrs. Rose when she fell ill."

"Christ, call her Jackie," Sissy said. "Every time you say Mrs. Rose, my brain seizes up. Yes, I was with her."

Ellen gripped Casey's arm. "She went to the hospital with Mom. Thank god she was there. I was too upset to think."

"Jackie was fine," Sissy said, wide-eyed. "Then, around seven, she started getting cramps. She's past needing Midol, so we figured it was something she ate. When the cramps got worse, I insisted that she talk to Ray."

"Ray?" Casey said.

"One of the vets that usually shows up for company shindigs."

"You consulted a vet? That was the first aid person?"

"Well, out of everyone there, I figured Ray would have the most educated guess about what to do," Sissy said haughtily. "When Jackie said her legs felt funny, he said we should go to emergency, and Mike agreed with him."

"Mike, her boss?"

Sissy nodded. "He insisted on driving us, helped Jackie down the stairs. I'm glad he was there, because we would have driven to St. Timothy's, which is closer. Mike told us about a bad experience there, and we didn't think it was an emergency, so we went to the General. Jackie kept suggesting that we just take her home, but Mike said she needed a doctor, and I agreed with him. She didn't look good."

"I didn't see Mike at the hospital," Ellen said.

"He was still there when you showed up. But the moment they said the word 'coma,' you almost fainted, remember? The doctor ushered you away. When I started blubbering, Mike went to see if he could get more information about your mother's condition. Or maybe he didn't know what to do. I don't know."

"Did he get more information?" Casey asked.

Sissy shifted her attention back to Casey. "I don't know. I didn't see him again that night. I waited for him to come back, but he never did, so I pulled myself together and found Ellen. She needed my support."

"I did, I did," Ellen agreed, nodding.

Maybe Sissy hadn't taken all that long to compose herself and go to Ellen. "How long did you wait for Mike?"

Sissy's brows drew together. "Oh, at least twenty minutes, maybe more. I figured he'd gone home, that he'd decided we didn't need him to stay."

"Did they check the food at the party?"

"They pumped her stomach and didn't find anything bad," Ellen said.

Casey looked down at her empty Danish wrapper. If she hadn't already finished it, the remains would be going in the garbage. "Did Jackie eat or drink anything that nobody else at the party ate or drank?"

"Not that I know of," Sissy said. "The doctor said it could have been something she'd eaten earlier that day, but they never explained the cramps, or the coma."

There was no point going back to the hospital, where Casey was persona non grata. She'd focus on the disappearance, rather than on the reason for Jackie's hospitalization. Who had kidnapped her, and why? "You said you noticed tension between Jackie and her boss. Do you know what that was about?"

"Nope."

Odd. She'd thought they were friends. "What exactly was Jackie working on?"

Sissy's answering gasp was so loud that it drew the attention of the couple at the next table. "I can't tell you that. It's classified. If a competitor found out . . ."

"I won't tell anyone."

"Sweetheart, when we agree to work for the company, we sign non-disclosure agreements that would make a lawyer's hair fall out. That's why I have no idea what was going on between Jackie and Mike. Jackie never discussed the details of her job with me. She wasn't allowed." Sissy pointed at herself with a long, manicured nail. "I'm an admin, not one of the scientists. Normally we don't talk with the white-coats much, but Jackie had social skills, you know, and she never looked down her nose at the rabble. We got to talking on a smoke break one day. Oh, I don't smoke anymore," she said, in response to Casey's disapproving frown. "I'm talking over twenty years ago, when Jackie and I used to stand outside freezing our asses off in the middle of winter. When we found out we both had daughters around the same age, we naturally became friends. But she never, ever told me anything that would violate her non-disclosure agreement."

"She didn't tell me much, either," Ellen said. "I found out she works on cat food because she brought home a sample for one of her old cats to try. I happened to be over that day. Projectile vomit everywhere. I wanted to rush him to the vet, but Mom said not to worry, and let it slip that she'd used him as a guinea pig. That was the one and only time she ever touched on what she does beyond that she develops cat foods."

Casey wanted to groan. A possible problem between Jackie and her boss was the only useful tidbit she'd gleaned over the last half-hour, but she'd put her chances of talking to Mike Hargrave at zero. This case was going nowhere in a hurry. "So you don't know anything about her situation at work."

"I didn't say that," Sissy said, making Casey want to punch her. "I don't know what she was working on, but I do know that morale was really low in her department. Not only that, someone was fired—well, laid off—a couple of weeks before the party. It was sudden. We all wondered whether he'd been caught stealing."

Could Jackie have ratted him out? Even if she had, kidnapping and killing her in retaliation would be a little extreme. "Do you have a way of contacting him? Do you think he'll talk to me?"

"I might be able to arrange that." Sissy cleared her throat. "Kenny has sort of a thing for me. We've spoken on the phone a few times since he left. He insists he did nothing wrong."

"If you could put us in touch, I'd appreciate it."

"I'll call him as soon as we're done. If I leave a message, it never takes him long to call me back," she said with a giggle.

"Was Jackie seeing anyone?" Casey asked, grasping at straws. "Maybe someone she didn't want her daughter to know about."

Ellen's face tightened. "Mom would never keep anything like that from me."

"Anyone, Sissy. If I'm going to find her . . ."

Sissy glanced at Ellen. "Nobody. There's nobody."

"Are you sure?" When Sissy nodded, Casey said, "If there's anything else you can think of that might help . . ."

Sissy shifted in her seat. "Well . . ."

"What?" Casey and Ellen said in unison.

"I saw Jackie in the main security office a few days before the party," she said, sounding apologetic.

"Is that unusual?" Casey asked.

"There are security stations all over our building, so there's no need to go to the main office. Still, I wouldn't have thought anything of it, except . . ." Casey and Ellen leaned forward ". . . I saw her in there again the day before the party." Sissy lowered her voice. "She was there when I was leaving, and I worked late that night. I don't think she wanted anyone to see her there."

"Did you ask her about it?"

Sissy shook her head. "Our friendship worked—works—because I didn't interrogate her about anything related to her job. We talked kids, clothes, men, the usual. Not work."

Casey leaned back. If Jackie's disappearance was related to her job, she didn't have a hope in hell of finding her. It sounded as if the pet food company had more security than an army base and guarded its secrets more diligently than a spy agency. "I guess I'll have a look through her purse now," she mumbled to Ellen, who dutifully lifted the purse from between her feet and plunked it on the table.

Under Ellen and Sissy's watchful eyes, Casey emptied the purse by lifting the items from it one by one and placing each item on the table. When she was satisfied that she'd found every pocket, nook, and cranny, she surveyed the purse's contents. A lady's wallet. A daily calendar. Empty gum wrappers. Some loose change. Several pens. A phone. "Did the police check her phone?"

"They didn't find anything," Ellen said. "Mom was a bit of a Luddite. She mainly used the phone to call me."

Since nothing else on the table leapt out at Casey, the purse was a dead end. "I don't see anything that will help." She moved to return the items to the purse, then stopped when Sissy suddenly shrieked, "Her notebook!"

Ellen's eyes bulged. She straightened. "You're right. Where is it?" She snatched the purse away from Casey and slid her fingers into its side pocket.

"I checked everywhere," Casey said. "Are you saying there's something missing?"

"Her notebook," Sissy said. "She never went anywhere without it."

"It was always tucked in here." Ellen felt around in the side pocket again.

"Jackie was always pulling it out and scribbling down ideas," Sissy explained. "She didn't have to worry about me or anyone else reading over her shoulder. I don't think anyone except her could understand her handwriting."

"When did you last see her with the notebook?" Casey asked.

Sissy's eyes grew distant. "A couple of hours before the party," she finally said. "Like I said, she was always writing in it."

"I didn't feel right about poking around in her purse, or I would have realized it was missing," Ellen said, plopping the purse back onto the table. "Okay, I might have borrowed a couple of dollars from her wallet, but I didn't check the side pockets. I had no reason to."

Casey considered the possibilities. "Could it have fallen out?"

"I don't think so."

"Who's had access to the purse, apart from the police?"

"Just me, and it's been locked away at home."

"What about the night she went to the hospital?" Casey asked Sissy.

"I had it with me the whole time."

"Did you ever put it down?"

"Sure, but only on the table next to my chair. I had my own purse to worry about, too."

Maybe Mike had taken the notebook. "Did everyone know about Jackie's habit of jotting down ideas?"

"Yep, she did it everywhere." Sissy's voice dropped again. "She even wrote in it in the ladies' room. In the stall."

Casey wouldn't ask how Sissy knew that useless bit of information. She self-consciously wrote notes in her own small notebook, then flipped it shut. "Do you think Mike would talk to me?"

Sissy drew back. "Talk to a PI? No!"

It had been worth a shot. "Thank you," Casey said to Sissy. "If you think of anything else . . ." Damn, she really needed to order business cards. "Let Ellen know. Oh, and don't forget to arrange a meeting with your, uh, friend. The fired guy."

"I'll call Kenny right now." Sissy pulled a phone from her purse, punched in a number, and held the phone to her ear. "Hey, it's me. Call me when you get a chance, okay?" She hung up and winked at Casey. "Don't worry, he'll call within the hour. What's your number?" As Casey recited it, Sissy added it to her contacts. "I wish I could be of more help." She dropped the phone into her purse and grabbed Casey's hand. "You'll find Jackie, right? I don't know what I'll do if we never find out what happened to her. How will we get on with our lives, knowing that Jackie is out there somewhere?"

"Oh my god, Mom," Ellen wailed. "Where are you, where are you?"

Sissy let go of Casey's hand and took Ellen in her arms. "Don't lose faith, Ellen. Don't lose faith."

Jesus, talk about pressure. Could she live with herself if she didn't find Jackie? When they visited the spa, they'd better leave with a solid lead or two, because Casey was running out of questions to ask and avenues to explore.

GRATEFUL THAT SISSY had come through and set up a meeting with the fired employee, Casey walked up the path to Kenny's house and rang the doorbell. She tried not to stare directly into the peephole as she waited. A deadbolt clicked, then the door swung open.

"Hi, you must be Casey." The man who held out his hand was at least ten years Sissy's junior.

Casey smiled and pumped his hand. "That's me."

"Come on in." He led her into a bright, airy living room and turned off the video game paused on the widescreen TV. "Want a drink?" he asked, motioning for her to sit down.

She chose the chair across from his obvious playing spot on the sofa. "No, thanks, I won't be staying long."

He moved a gamepad from the sofa to the coffee table and sat down. "So Sissy told you about me, eh?"

Casey nodded.

Kenny stretched his arm across the back of the sofa. "Does she talk about me much?"

"I don't really know her," Casey said, her slight apprehension about meeting him alone in his house going out the window. He had eyes for one woman, and one woman only. "I'm working for Ellen Myers, Jackie Rose's daughter."

"Yeah, Sissy mentioned that."

"When she told me you were fired—"

"Laid off," Kenny said, wagging his finger. "And anything you've heard about me stealing is bullshit. Look." Leaning forward, he lifted a pile of papers from the coffee table and held them toward Casey.

She slid to the edge of her chair, then rose when she realized the sheets were out of reach. Back in her chair, she scanned the top sheet. "These are your termination papers."

"Right. And if you read through them, you'll see there's no mention of stealing. That's just a vicious rumour Jim started. He noticed that Sissy and I were growing . . . close, so when I was laid off—boom, he moves in and starts spreading lies." Kenny moistened his lips. "Didn't work, though. Sissy didn't turn her back on me and run to him, like he expected."

Cripes, it sounded like Sissy was the stud magnet at work.

"Them laying me off was bullshit, too. Downsizing, my ass. If they're downsizing, why was I let go instead of Dan? He's only been there a couple of years."

Casey skimmed Kenny's papers as he droned on. Yep, it did say they'd let him go because they were reorganizing and didn't have another suitable position for him. Kenny had a good point. Why him?

"If they're strapped for cash, why all the new hires? Not long before I was laid off, there was one guy who'd just joined the canine development department, a new gal in admin, and a new security guard."

Casey perked up. "Security guard?"

Kenny nodded. "Yeah, and according to Sissy, the guy didn't stick around very long. Maybe he was laid off, too. Good riddance. Kept telling me to stop using the fire exit that led right to where my car was parked. I'd used it for years before that asshole came along."

"Did he leave before or after Jackie collapsed?"

"I don't know." Kenny scratched his cheek. "After, I think, but I'm not sure."

"Is there a high turnover in security?"

Kenny shrugged. "How should I know? Like I said, I only noticed the guy because he was so anal. What's the big deal about the security guard?"

She was probably trying to see connections that weren't there. "If you don't believe the reorganization reason they gave you, why do you think they let you go?"

"I pissed someone off. Problem is, I don't know who. But they were clever. They couldn't fire me, so they reorged my ass out of the department, instead."

If that was true, it had to be Mike Hargrave or one of his superiors. "Can you tell me anything about Jackie's work? Or about the problems in the department?"

Kenny's eyes narrowed. "I'm sure Sissy mentioned the non-disclosure agreement." He pointed at the paper pile on Casey's lap. "Hell, I'm not even supposed to show you those, but for Sissy . . ."

Casey suppressed a snort, then wanted to kick herself. He hadn't set up this meeting to help her. He wanted to further his cause with Sissy and find out what Sissy was saying about him. She'd give him a point for backing up his doubts about his dismissal with paperwork, but he'd better have more for her than that. "You sure you don't know who you pissed off? Did anything strange happen at work before you left?"

Kenny scrunched up his face. "Nope. In fact, things were going well. I'd been putting in extra hours working on our next formula. I deserved a raise, not the boot."

"So you were going in early—"

"No, working late. I'm not a morning person."

Had he seen something after hours that he wasn't supposed to see? Her gut told her that Kenny had just told her something important. Then again, it could be the tortilla she'd had for lunch. "When you were working late, did you see anyone who wasn't supposed to be around?"

"Nope. Just people in our department."

"Did anything weird happen?"

"Nope."

Maybe it *was* the tortilla. "Do you know if Jackie had any health problems? Food allergies, maybe?"

"She kept to herself. Well, she was good friends with Sissy, but everyone likes Sissy."

Apparently. Casey let out an exaggerated sigh. "I was hoping you could tell me something that would help me find Jackie. Sissy's *really* upset over this. Really, really upset. She'll be so grateful to anyone who gives me the information that cracks the case."

"Grateful, eh?"

"Really, really grateful."

Kenny rubbed his lower lip. "You might want to speak to Donna Wilkins. She's Mike's boss."

"What good would that do? I'm sure she signed the same non-disclosure agreement you did."

"She's a gossip. She won't divulge company secrets, but she might let slip a few details about the office politics in our department."

"Or you could just tell me." Casey moved the papers to the coffee table and leaned forward. "Nobody will know you said anything."

Kenny shook his head. "I'm on shakier ground than Donna. That fat severance I got? If I violate the agreement in any way, shape, or form, they can ask for it back. I'm not risking it. I need the money. Got a nice getaway planned for me and Sissy. A surprise."

It would certainly be a surprise for Sissy. "I wouldn't rush it," she said. "I'd ask her to dinner first. Get to know each other a little more, outside of work." Give Sissy a chance to figure out whether she wanted to do more than flirt with Kenny on the phone.

He almost leapt off the sofa. "Did she drop a hint about dinner?" He stared at her, his muscles taut.

"A subtle one." Not saying anything at all was about as subtle as one could get. "Sissy's the sort that would like to be wined and dined for a while." Or maybe Casey was projecting. "At least tell her in person about the getaway." He remained motionless. She could hear his wheels turning. "Anyway, getting back to Donna, I'm sure her lips are only loose with her work colleagues."

"Nah, she loves to dish. She won't give away anything important, but you're not interested in food formulas, anyway."

"How am I supposed to even talk to her?"

"This is where you owe me. Big. This is what I want in ret—"

"Make sure Sissy knows you helped me out. Deal. Now, spill." Casey folded her arms.

Kenny smirked. "Donna's into cats. She'll be showing one of her best at the annual dog and cat fair next weekend. Kills two birds with one stone. Shows the cat, talks up the food. Drop in on her there, compliment her feline, and get her talking."

Casey had never understood cat shows. Cats were supposed to be independent, aloof, have attitude. No respectable cat would fawn for an audience, especially when its owner wanted it to. But she could think of worse field trips than traipsing around a cat and dog show for an afternoon. "You mean the show at the downtown convention centre?"

"That's the one," Kenny said with a nod. "You want a ticket? I scored a bunch of complimentary ones a couple of days before they axed me."

"Not to be greedy, but can I have two?"

"Why not?"

"Great." She'd take Gran. The role of doting granddaughter might earn her trust points.

"Just make sure you talk me up to Sissy, okay?"

"I will." Casey meant it. Finding out how to chat with Mike Hargrave's boss had made the half-hour bus ride more than worth it.

Chapter Five

"So, remember, we don't want them to know that we think the contest might have been a sham," Casey said to Ellen as they pulled into Radiant Rejuvenations' parking lot. "They might not even know of any contest. The weekend could have been a gift. Did you tell them you were a contest winner when you checked in?"

Ellen pulled down the driver's visor and fished a lipstick from her purse. "I don't remember." She gazed into the mirror clipped to the visor and touched up her lips. "There was a congratulatory basket in my room, though."

"Anybody could have sent that." Casey climbed out of the car and followed Ellen to the entrance . . . and into an oasis. The sun streaming through the windows, the water fountain, the plants, the white cushioned benches, the cooled air . . . How much did a night here cost? If someone had paid for Ellen's stay out of pocket, he hadn't spared any expense.

A man in skimpy swimming trunks and flip-flops smiled as he strolled past. Ellen turned and lifted her sunglasses. "Nice butt."

"The front desk," Casey said.

"Don't be a spoilsport," Ellen murmured, but she lowered her sunglasses and approached Reception, with Casey trailing after her.

Could she trust Ellen to be subtle? Was the sky green? Maybe she should have tried her own luck before involving anyone else. A quick glance around the reception area indicated that most of the clientele were women over forty, but another twenty-something beach boy looked up when they approached the desk. Whatever floated their boats.

"Can I help you?" the young man said.

Ellen smiled. "I stayed here about a month and a half ago."

Beach boy grinned back at her. "Really? I mustn't have been working, because I would have remembered you."

Ellen's hand went to her throat. "I'm sure you say that to everyone." Casey concurred.

"Only the lovely ones," beach boy said smoothly. "Are you back for another stay?" His eyes flicked to Casey. "This time with your sister?"

"My sister?" Ellen giggled. "Oh, no, no, no." She coyly eyed him. "How could you think she's my sister? I'm old enough to be her mother."

Beach boy drew back and placed his hand on his chest. "No way. You don't look a day over thirty."

Casey wanted to roll her eyes. These two couldn't possibly believe the BS coming out of their mouths, right?

"She's a friend I brought with me for moral support," Ellen said. "I'm hoping you can help get someone off my back."

Beach boy's brow furrowed. "Who?"

"You won't believe this. I won a contest for a weekend stay here. The company took care of everything, of course, and I enjoyed every minute. Every single minute. Unfortunately, I left without a copy of the bill, which was apparently a really dumb thing to do. Can you believe I have to pay tax on that win? My accountant needs to know the dollar value of my stay."

"I didn't know you had to declare that sort of thing," beach boy said.

"Oh, yes. Bloodsuckers, all of them. Everyone wants a piece of you." Ellen held out her arm and pinched it. "Christ, they tax you when you die, too. You'd figure they'd give you a pass on that, but nope. They don't care that you're six feet under."

Beach boy's eyes widened. "So you want a copy of the bill?"

"Please. I contacted the contest company, and they said it would take months to get it from the accounting department. The woman said to get it from here instead, that it would be faster."

"What's your name?"

"Ellen Myers. *Miss* Ellen Myers."

Casey held her breath as beach boy tapped away at the reception computer's keyboard and gazed at the screen. "You stayed in the Dawnlight Suite. Wow, that was some prize. Normally contest winners get one of our lower priced suites."

"I absolutely loved it," Ellen said. "But now I'm nervous. How much tax is this going to cost me?"

"I'll print a copy of the bill for you." He pressed a key and disappeared through a doorway behind the desk. Casey heard the familiar hum of a laser printer producing a page.

"How am I doing?" Ellen whispered.

"Not now. You'll give yourself away."

Ellen covered her mouth and turned back to the counter.

Casey nudged her. "Don't forget to ask about Trudy," she whispered.

Hmm, the printer had fallen silent, but beach boy hadn't returned. Seconds stretched to minutes. Casey resisted the urge to dig her fingernails into Ellen's arm. Was beach boy consulting with a superior? Was he calling the contact person on the bill, which would be disastrous? Was he combing his hair? She almost fainted with relief when he returned to the counter and handed a paper to Ellen.

"I had to blacken out some details—you know, the credit card number, that sort of thing," he said, explaining the dark lines on the page.

"No problem." Ellen folded the paper and slipped it into her purse's side pocket. "Thank you. This will help get my accountant off my back." She sighed. "Maybe you could do me one more teeny-tiny favour."

"Lay it on me."

"I met someone while I was here. Trudy Michaels. Unfortunately I lost her phone number and email address. Could you—"

Beach boy shook his head. "I'm sorry. I can't give out information about other guests."

Oh well, it had been worth a try.

He smiled at Ellen and leaned over the counter. "Are you sure you don't want a massage while you're here?"

Ellen simpered. "Will you be giving it?"

Wanting to get out of there already, Casey fought the urge to kick Ellen.

"Unfortunately, no."

"Too bad. I'll have to say no this time, then."

"Thanks for helping us." Casey moved away from the counter and hoped that Ellen would follow.

Once outside, she wanted to snatch the copied bill from Ellen's purse, but she restrained herself until they were in the car. "Can I see it?"

A grin split Ellen's face. "Did you see that? He didn't even blink. He just made the copy and handed it over." She touched Casey's arm. "That was fun. Maybe we can work together on other cases."

"Maybe," Casey said. "Can I see it?"

"What?"

"The bill."

Ellen's mouth formed an O. She pulled the bill from her purse's pocket and handed it to Casey, who eagerly unfolded it. Excitement surged through her. Beach boy had crossed out everything, but she could still make out a name and phone number. "Do you know an Aaron Street?"

"Where is it? In this town?"

"No, Aaron Street is the name of the guy who booked your weekend."

"Oh." Ellen's brow furrowed. She shook her head. "Never heard of him. What now?"

"Leave this with me," Casey said, refolding the paper and slipping it into her back pocket. Finally, a break in the case—assuming Aaron Street didn't work for a company that ran contests for its clients.

CASEY TYPED AARON Street's phone number into the appropriate field and did a reverse lookup. Hmm . . . B. Gardner, with a local address. Was Aaron Street a partner, a roommate, a boarder, or a fake name? Searching the Net and social networks turned up plenty of hits, but none with his address. The guy was an online ghost. Fake name, then? But how had he obtained a credit card tied to the address? Maybe he was a Luddite. Gran couldn't be found online, and she certainly existed.

Rather than calling the number to see who answered, Casey decided to scope out the address. The next day, she got off the bus and strolled up Pine Avenue, which led to Maple Drive, where Aaron Street supposedly lived. Maple Drive turned out to be a four-lane road, though parked cars meant only two could be used for driving. Casey wouldn't be conspicuous; too many people walked, jogged, and pushed strollers for her to stand out. Gardner's house was number 562. She slowed her pace when she passed number 558, then 560, then 562. A house, not a store or empty lot. She kept going until she reached a traffic light, then crossed the road, doubled back, and tied her shoelace across from number 562. Nothing set the house apart from its neighbours, and she could pretend to tie her shoelace all day and not see anyone enter or leave the residence. Now that she knew it was a house, she'd call.

Around the corner, she pulled out her phone and dialed Street's—Gardner's—number. "Hello?" a female voice said.

"Can I speak to Mr. Street, please?" Casey said.

A pause, then, "Let me guess. You'll also want to speak to Mr. Boulevard, or Mr. Avenue. And yes, my fridge is running, and no, I'm not going to catch it. Bugger off."

"Wait! I'm not—" The line went dead.

Great. She redialed the number, but this time it went through to voice mail. Freaking call display. She'd hoped to avoid knocking on the door, but now she had no choice. Two minutes later, she rang the doorbell and waited.

The door opened. A woman in a t-shirt and sweats gave Casey the once-over. "Yeah?"

"I'm looking for Aaron Street. I tried calling, but . . ."

"That was you? Why the hell didn't you just say Aaron Street in the first place?"

"You know him?"

"No, I just think it was stupid to call up and ask for Mr. Street." The woman's hand went to her hip. "Didn't you ever make prank phone calls when you were a kid?"

"Uh, not really."

"Oh. Well, not that I'd know much about it. There's the fridge one, and the running nose variation." The woman's eyes grew distant. "Oh, and the one where you call and ask for Mr. Smith, and after doing that a few times, you have someone call and say, 'This is Mr. Smith. Are there any messages for me?'" She slapped her thigh and laughed.

Casey faked a chuckle. "Do you know Aaron Street?"

"Aaron . . . Street, did you say?"

"Yeah."

The woman shook her head. "Never heard of him."

"You sure?"

"Yes, I'm damn sure. Does he owe someone money or something? Are you a debt collector?" Her eyes narrowed. "As far as I'm concerned, they're all cold-blooded, cold-hearted bastards—or bitches, as the case may be."

"No, I'm not." And she wasn't about to tell the woman that she was a private investigator. "Aaron is, uh, my ex. He used to live here, or at least he told me he did. We weren't together very long. It's really important that I find him."

The woman's eyes widened. "Oh my god, honey, did he knock you up? That bastard! I wish you'd told me right away. I know him, okay? We're not close friends or anything. I even forgot his damn last name. He's my hubby's brother-in-law's sister-in-law's brother. He stayed with us for a couple of months." She pointed to the ground. "In the basement. Moved out a couple of weeks ago, but I don't know where. Hubby dealt with him, not me. I can find out, though. The bastard. Never liked him. I don't even know why hubby wanted to help him. It's not like Aaron is related to us or anything. Give me your name and number. He needs to do right by you."

"Sure," Casey said, uncomfortable with the idea of the woman thinking she was pregnant, but elated that she was willing to help. She pulled out her notebook, scribbled her name and number, and tore off the page. "Here." She handed it to the woman. "I really appreciate your help."

"I'll call you." The door closed.

Casey walked back to the bus stop. The afternoon hadn't been a total loss. The woman might come through, or she might speak to Street and figure out that there was no pregnant girlfriend. If that happened, maybe Detective Walker could help find Street, or maybe she'd tell Casey to buzz off. All Casey could do was bide her time and hope for a call.

CASEY GROANED WHEN she emerged from the grocery store, her knapsack packed with milk, cat food, and soup. The weather channel had said a thirty percent chance of showers, but the sky said a ninety-five percent chance. Muttering under her breath about inaccurate weather reports, she unlocked her bike. Maybe she should have taken the bus, but come on; thirty percent usually meant it wouldn't rain.

She was about to pedal when her phone rang. "Hello."

"Hey, it's Sissy. Sorry I didn't call you back yesterday. I was at Kenny's and, uh, by the time I left it was, um, too late to call."

Too early, more like. "No problem. Did he tell you that he mentioned a security guard?"

"No," Sissy drawled.

"He mentioned a new guard who didn't stay around long. You mentioned Jackie visiting security a couple of times. I was just wondering if you saw who she was speaking with, and whether it was that guard."

Sissy snorted. "Casey, I just happened to see her go into the security office a couple of times. I wasn't spying on her. I didn't rush up to the window and watch. Especially since . . ."

"Since what?" Casey prompted.

"Well, I thought maybe she was going in there because she was interested in someone, which, believe me, would have been the first time in a while. I didn't want to spook her by breathing down her neck. I figured she'd tell me in her own time."

"But you don't know that for sure."

"No."

"Does security have a high turnover?"

"I have no idea," Sissy said. "When I smoked, I used to chat with the guards. Now I hardly notice them. I couldn't even tell you most of their names. Why?"

She was trying to put two and two together, connect the dots, tie some random guard's start and end dates with Jackie's disappearance. It was called "being desperate." "It doesn't matter," she said to Sissy, then glanced up at the sky and quietly swore. "I have to go. Thanks for calling back."

She slid her phone into her pocket and pushed into motion. *Ten minutes. Please, rain, hold off for ten minutes . . .*

Two minutes later, the skies opened. Rain dripping from her nose, Casey waited for a light to change while trying to look as if sitting on her bike, drenched, was perfectly okay with her. Yep, all those dry motorists were staring out their windshields, thinking, *Thank god it's not me,* as they listened to the windshield wipers thump back and forth. At least her helmet was keeping her hair dry.

The light changed. Casey had just cleared the intersection when a van slowed next to her. Shit. She hated it when drivers wouldn't pass, even though they had plenty of room. A horn sounded, making her jump. *Hey, I'm practically scraping the curb, here!* When the driver honked again, Casey twisted to look, hoping she wouldn't stare into the eyes of a deranged anti-cyclist determined to take back the road for motorists. The driver waved and motioned for Casey to stop. She squinted through the rain. Emily?

Casey braked, then cautiously rolled up to the driver's side door after Emily pulled over in front of her. The window whirred down. Emily smiled up at her. "I thought it was you. Didn't you see me waving at the light?"

"Uh, no."

"Want a lift?"

Casey glanced down at her bike.

"It'll fit in the back."

"I'm soaked."

"Who cares? It's my father's van. Come on, put your bike in the back and get in."

Casey opened her mouth to protest, then inwardly shrugged and dismounted. Emily had unlocked the side door. After laying her bike down in the back next to stacks of unmarked boxes, Casey climbed into the passenger seat and plunked her knapsack on her lap, but kept her helmet on. No way was she removing her helmet. When Emily glanced at her, Casey cleared her throat. "Do you usually ride in torrential rain?" Emily asked as she waited to merge into traffic.

"Not intentionally. The weather report said there was only a thirty percent chance of showers."

Emily grunted.

"The sky looked fine when I left."

"The storm blew in quickly."

She silently thanked Emily for not making her feel like an idiot. "So this is your father's van?" she said, wanting to avoid awkward silence and unwanted personal questions.

"Yeah. I should have known he wanted me to do something when he asked me to drop by the shop. Though it's not his fault. Someone booked off sick, so I'm playing delivery girl." They turned a corner. "You're in that complex on the corner of Second, right?"

"Yeah." Gran must have told her.

"Where do you keep your bike?"

"There's a storage room in the basement."

"I see."

"Where do you live?" Casey asked.

"Near the university. Since I work the early morning shift, it would make more sense for me to live near the shop. But when I found the apartment, things were different."

"You worked the later shift."

Emily was silent for a moment, then said, "Yes."

Was there more? She didn't want to pry, and Emily was already pulling up in front of her apartment building. They hadn't been that far away when Emily had picked her up, a gesture she'd probably regret when she saw the wet seat. "Thanks for the ride."

Emily turned to her. "Any time." She paused. "Maybe I'll see you in the shop soon."

"Maybe you will," Casey said, figuring the chances she'd be in the shop that early in the morning were nil. But she appreciated Emily's willingness to shuttle a drowned rat home. "Your shop has the best server in town. You're sweeter than the Danishes." She froze when Emily's face flushed a deep red. Oh my god. She hadn't meant—she never flirted with straight women. "Thanks again," she mumbled, and scrambled out of the van. Despite wanting to get away, she couldn't help but look at the seat. "Sorry," she said, wincing.

Emily chuckled. "It's just water. And it's still raining. You'd better go."

Especially since it was raining into the van. Casey slammed the door shut and slung her knapsack over her shoulder. She pulled her bike from the back of the van, then peered into the passenger window and waved. Emily returned the gesture and pulled away, probably glad to be rid of her wet, flirty passenger. Next time she saw Casey in the rain, she'd drive by, making sure to hit a deep puddle for good measure.

MUNCHING ON A sandwich, Casey reviewed her notes, desperate to spot a clue that she'd missed the first four times she'd read them over. She'd visited Aaron Street's former residence three days ago, but no call. She could call the woman, but she didn't want to be a pest, or be accused of harassment. So, what next? Call Detective Walker? Casey dreaded begging her to help.

Gran stared down at her empty plate. "I think I'll have some ice cream. Do you want some?"

Casey shook her head.

"No ice cream? What's the matter?" Gran shouted.

"I'm not in the mood. And will you please turn on your hearing aids?" Casey asked, motioning next to her ear. "For me? Please." When Gran dutifully complied, Casey blew out an exasperated sigh. "Sorry, I know I'm being pissy, but I don't want to blow my first case. I need to know I can do this." Her eyes welled with tears. She looked down at her notebook again. "Why did it have to be a missing comatose woman? How many freaking comatose people go missing? I don't even have other cases I can consult. I did a search on the Net. Nothing. Comatose people are usually accounted for, you know?"

Gran tutted and pulled a tub of ice cream from the freezer. "You must have gathered some clues."

"Yes, I have, and they've all been dead ends. Every time I look into something, bam! Brick wall." She grabbed her head. "She has to be somewhere."

"You'll figure it out. Pretend you're one of those detectives on TV."

"That won't help. It's TV! They lift fingerprints from freaking water on TV." She jabbed a finger onto her notebook. "This is real life."

Gran frowned. "I'm talking about the reality cop shows," she said as she sat down with her bowl of ice cream.

"Have you noticed that it's tipsters and surveillance camera footage that usually give them the breaks, not a trail of obvious clues leading right to the culprit's front door?" Casey's phone rang. She snatched it up from the table. "Hello."

"Casey?"

Her heart leapt into her mouth. "Yes."

"This is Tina. You came to my place a few days ago about Aaron."

She held her breath.

"Who is it?" Gran asked. Casey brought a finger to her lips and shook her head.

"I've got his address and phone number," Tina said. "You want it?"

"Yes!" Casey suppressed a whoop and wrote down the details in her notebook. "Thanks, I really appreciate it."

"Sorry it took so long. Hubby had to pry it out of his brother-in-law." Tina paused. "Now, listen. When I told hubby what Aaron had done to you, he hit the damn roof. Turns out he hated the prick, too. Hubby boxed in high school and has a brown belt in karate. He's going to head over there and beat the shit out of the twerp. You want to watch?"

"What? No! Don't do that."

"Casey. Honey. Grow a damn backbone. You can't let the prick get away with what he did. If someone doesn't teach him a lesson, he'll knock up some other poor girl."

Shit! "Tina . . . he may be a prick, but . . . he's the father of my baby."

Gran's eyes bulged. The ice cream on the way to her mouth dropped onto her shirt. "Holy shit, when did that happen?" she bellowed. "I thought you were a lesbian!"

"What?" Tina said.

Casey glared at Gran and pushed back her chair. "Nothing," she said as she left the kitchen. "You heard the TV. Some soap opera." *Called my life.* "Tina, I appreciate what your husband wants to do, but I'd like Aaron to be coherent when I talk to him."

"You sure?"

"Yeah. How else will I get money out of him?"

"Good point. Okay, Casey, but if you change your mind, call me back, okay?"

"Thanks, Tina. Oh, one more question. Do you know Trudy Michaels?"

"Never heard of her. Is she another one of Aaron's conquests? Bastard."

"Uh, no. Thanks anyway. Bye." Casey hung up, shoved her phone into her pocket, and turned around.

Gran stood in the kitchen archway, dabbing at her shirt with a napkin. She sighed and looked up. "Look at this mess."

"I'm not pregnant." Casey tossed her notebook onto the nearby end table and threw her hands into the air. "How could you believe I'm pregnant?"

"It sounded like you're pregnant to me," Gran said indignantly.

"I was undercover. I had to pretend some guy was my ex-boyfriend, so his ex-landlord would tell me where I could find him."

"Well, that's a relief. Christ, I only just got used to you being a lesbian. Though I suppose that doesn't mean you'll never get pregnant." Gran pointed at the TV. "I saw a show about a lesbian couple that had a baby. One of their friends donated the sperm. He did his thing and then brought the goods to their house in a bottle. Stuck it up her whatsit using a turkey baster, if you can believe that." Her eyes widened. "A delivery guy was here not too long ago."

Casey rolled her eyes. "Books, Gran. Books. Do you really think I'd have sperm delivered through UPS?"

"You never know."

"Plus, that was only a week ago. I wouldn't know if I'm pregnant yet." What a bizarre conversation. Seriously. "Do you really think I'd want to get pregnant now, when I'm single and just starting a new career? And don't you think I'd discuss it with you first? After all, you'd be the kid's other mom." She batted her eyelashes at Gran and grinned.

"Bah." Gran waved a dismissive hand. "You're too young to have a baby anyway. You're still a baby yourself."

"I'm twenty-three."

"Twenty-three today is the equivalent of fourteen in my day," Gran said with a wag of her finger. "When I was twenty-three, I was married with two kids. These days, kids are still at home when they're thirty. You can't get rid of them."

Casey's hands went to her hips. "Do you want me to move out?"

"No! You don't live with your mom and dad. You live with your gran."

"To some people, that's the same thing."

"Not in this case. We help each other out, right? Right?"

"I suppose so," Casey mumbled.

Gran held out her arms. "Come here."

Casey shook her head and went to her, then gasped for air when Gran held her tight. A moment later, she drew back, mollified. "At least I have a lead now," she said, picking up the notebook. "But with the way things are going, it'll probably be a dead end."

"Don't think like that. You just got your big break." Gran touched the side of her nose. "I can feel it."

"I hope you're right." Casey pulled out her phone to call Street, but went into her bedroom and closed the door before she dialed the number.

Chapter Six

Casey rode up to the bike rack outside the coffee shop and peered through the front window as she secured her bike. The shop was packed, but she immediately spotted Street. Not many in the noonday crowd had purple hair.

She walked over to his table. "Hey."

Street looked up from his cup. "Oh, hey. You Casey?"

She nodded.

"Want a coffee?"

"No, that's okay, thanks." She sat down across from him. "Thanks for agreeing to meet."

"Hey, no problem. When Tina called and said I'd better talk to you, I told her, no problem. Anything for Tina. Miss those guys, man. Miss them. We were like family." He stared morosely down at his cup again, then lifted his head. "She mentioned something about a baby?"

"A baby?" Casey forced a surprised expression. "She must have heard me wrong. No, no baby."

"That's good, because I think I'd remember a night with you." He raised an appraising eyebrow. "You seeing anyone?"

Ugh. "I'm a single mother. Three kids. Had my first one when I was fifteen. Wouldn't mind another one."

His face fell. She stifled a grin. "Listen, one of my friends won a spa weekend, and we're trying to get in touch with the contest promoters because there's a problem with the bill. It was supposed to be all-inclusive, but the spa is hitting her up for her drinks." Which would probably bankrupt Ellen, if it were true.

Street's eyes grew wary. "Hey, I don't know anything about no bill."

Casey tutted. "Your former phone number is on it, and I assume it's your credit card number, too. If you don't help me out, we'll sue you for misrepresenting the terms of the weekend."

"Hey!"

"What company do you work for?" One of the items beach boy had crossed out could be a company name, but Street didn't know that. "The name was conveniently left off the bill, probably because you knew you were going to stiff the winner."

Street held up his hands. "I had nothing to do with that. I don't work for no contest promoter. I answered an ad, okay?"

"An ad?"

"Yeah, on one of those classifieds sites on the Net. It sounded like easy money, and it was. All I had to do was put something on my credit card in exchange for the cash. I didn't know the guy was planning to stiff the lady, okay? I thought it was his wife."

Casey sighed and pulled out her notebook. "Start at the beginning. Tell me the truth, and I'll make sure my friend doesn't include your name in the court case."

Street drained his cup and plunked it on the table. "Like I said, I answered an ad. All I had to do was call the spa and book a weekend package on my credit card. He said it was a surprise for his wife. He didn't want it on his card because she reviews his statements like a hawk."

"Did he tell you to pretend it was for a contest winner?"

"Yeah. Gave me the name of some company. It's not my fault it's not on the bill."

"What was the name?"

"I don't know."

Casey gave him what she hoped was an intimidating glare. "You don't know."

"Hey, why would I remember the name? I did what he wanted, got my dough, and left. I didn't have to take a fucking test."

"What about the wife's name?"

"I don't remember it."

"Do you remember your own name?"

His face tightened. "I think her last name was different to his. I remember thinking she must be one of those feminist bi—uh, ladies."

"It didn't cross your mind that she might not be his wife?" Casey would have assumed they were having an affair. "How far in advance did you book the weekend?"

Street rubbed his chin. "About two weeks beforehand. But his wife could see his transactions online, you know."

If there was a wife who cared about his transactions, Casey would be flabbergasted. "Okay, so you met the guy, where?"

"In a parking lot, about eleven p.m."

Street was an idiot. "You made the call, he handed you the cash, and your business was done."

Street nodded.

"How much cash?"

"A few thousand," Street mumbled.

"A few thousand?" The spa wasn't *that* fancy. "In cash?"

"Yeah."

The man Street had met was an idiot, too, unless he was someone who could take care of himself. "So he gave you a little extra."

"Hey, I was doing the guy a favour. He promised me I'd only be on the hook for the reservation." Street pointed at himself. "I'm the one who was stiffed, here. He didn't mention booze. He also said I'd be in trouble if I cancelled the weekend. The guy was shifty. I wasn't about to cross him. I got good instincts."

Casey resisted the impulse to roll her eyes. "If you had good instincts, maybe you would have thought twice about meeting some dude alone at night, and asking more questions might have helped, too. Does the guy have a name?"

"Yeah, but I don't remember it."

Of course he didn't. "What did he look like?"

Street screwed up his face. "It was dark."

"Not dark enough that you couldn't read your credit card details. Come on."

"Hey, I wasn't interested in the guy, you know."

"Hair colour. Height. Build. Anything!" Casey said with a sigh. Then she scribbled down the meagre details Street provided. Unfortunately she'd have to run them by Walker. "You said you contacted him online. How?"

"Email."

"Do you still have the emails?"

"Probably."

"I want them. They're the only proof you have that this guy actually exists."

Street folded his arms. "Give me a fucking break. Why would I make up a story? I haven't done anything wrong."

"Uh, my friend is on the hook for her drinks and extras."

"Hey, I'm the victim here."

"You won't mind helping me find the guy, then. I want those emails."

Street scowled and pulled out his smartphone. "What's your email address?"

Casey printed it and turned her notebook around. Street squinted at it as he tapped away at his phone. "John Smith."

"John Smith?"

"Yeah, that was the guy's name."

Sure it was. Jesus, if the mystery man had said his name was John Doe, Street wouldn't have blinked.

"You know, the guy might have been a cop," Street said.

"You said he was shifty."

"He might have been shifty because he knew he was doing something wrong. I don't know, it was the look, the posture, the suit."

"You knew you were doing something wrong."

Street jerked his head up. "I thought it was strange, but it was easy money. The guy didn't ask to see my credit card, nothing. So I figured it was risk free. I didn't do anything illegal."

"Wrong isn't always illegal."

Street grunted and slipped his phone back into his jacket pocket. "Done."

Casey checked her email to make sure Street hadn't sent her a bunch of spam. "Thank you."

"That's all you're getting. I didn't stiff your friend. If she wants to sue me, tell her to go ahead. I don't have any money."

"Burned through the few grand already, eh?"

"Fuck you."

Casey flipped her notebook shut and slid it into her pocket, along with her pen. "See you around."

Street squinted up at her. "Hey, that spa weekend cost almost a grand. That room was like four fucking hundred dollars a night. It probably cost twenty fucking bucks for a glass of wine."

"That's why my friend is pissed. And while we're on the subject, do you know Trudy Michaels?"

"Is that your friend's name? I've never heard of her, I swear. It wasn't anything personal."

"You sure you don't know her?"

"Scout's honour."

Casey snorted. "Thanks for your help." She quickly left. God, she hoped she'd never run into Tina. To think that Tina thought she'd dated the moron—and was pregnant with his baby. Cripes.

As she unlocked her bike, she pondered what to do next. She could read the emails on her phone, but it was already late afternoon. She might as well read them at home.

Half an hour later, she sat at the computer in her bedroom and read through the handful of forwarded emails. They confirmed Street's story, but didn't offer any other clues. Maybe "John Smith's" email address could lead her to him, but how? She didn't know anyone who—coffee shop! Emily. She'd said she was doing a PhD in computer science. She'd also said she worked the early shift. Casey would have to drag herself out of bed and try to catch Emily before her shift was over.

Okay, she had a plan to deal with the emails. Next . . . she glanced down at her open notebook, then found Detective Walker's card and dialed her number.

"Casey who?" Walker said when Casey said her name.

"Casey Cook. You had lunch with me. I'm looking into Jacqueline Rose's disappearance."

"Oh, the kid detective." Walker snickered. "I'm only joking. I knew who you were."

Hilarious. "Do you have the description of Steve Rose handy?"

"Why?"

"I think the spa weekend Ellen Myers went on was bogus."

"The spa weekend?"

Did Walker even remember the freaking case? "She was there when Mrs. Rose went missing."

"Right. Why do you think it's bogus? The spa's legit. We called it."

"She said she won the weekend through a contest. I think she was set up. There was no contest."

"Oh, so the *contest* was bogus." Walker tutted. "You have to be precise in this business. Why do you think the contest was bogus?"

"Because some low-life booked the stay for someone he met through an online ad site."

"Really?"

"Yeah, and I want to see if his description of the guy he met matches Steve Rose's description."

"Describe him."

Casey hesitated.

"Hello? What did he look like?"

Sure. She'd tell Walker, who'd then grunt and hang up. But what choice did she have? "About six foot one, Caucasian, dark hair, crew cut, muscular build."

"Yeah, that could be the same guy. But it could be thousands of other guys in the city, too."

"But it could be him," Casey said, her gut telling her that mystery man and Steve Rose were one and the same. "Thanks."

"Whoa! Don't hang up. How did you find out about the ad?"

"I got a receipt from the spa and tracked down the guy who owned the credit card."

"Not bad, not bad," Walker said, her tone conveying approval—and surprise. "Drop everything you have off at Station 22, okay? I want it here by tomorrow noon."

"Do you have an email address? I can scan and email everything."

"Casey, it's on my business card."

Right. Oh well, it was nice to have Walker's respect for fifteen seconds. "I'm still going to look into this."

"Be my guest. But be careful, okay? You can always call me if you want me to deal with someone."

"Yeah, sure. Oh, Ellen Myers met someone named Trudy Michaels at the spa. Michaels could have been a plant. When I search the Net, there are hundreds of Trudy Michaels."

"So you want me to, what, get a warrant to obtain her details from the spa? Based on what? A PI having a hunch? Do you have anything solid—you know, that thing called evidence?"

"Uh, no."

"Later." The line went dead.

Casey stared at her phone. Walker had a way of making her feel two feet tall. Why couldn't another detective have been sympathetic to Ellen's plight? Why not a kind, generous detective who'd take Casey under his wing and pass down his wisdom—like on TV!

Shaking her head at herself, she typed her notes from her meeting with Street into an email, attached the scanned spa receipt, and hit Send. If the information somehow led Walker to Jackie, Walker would take all the credit. Okay, enough dumping on the detective. At least she was open to talking to the "kid detective." Ellen's retainer and a detective's business card in her pocket wouldn't be a bad haul from Casey's first case, but finding Jackie would be sweeter.

Her phone rang. "Hello."

"Casey Cook?" a male said.

"Yes?"

His voice became friendlier. "Hi. This is Mike Hargrave. I worked—work—with Jackie."

"Right. Ellen Myers mentioned you," Casey said, keeping her tone neutral.

"Sissy told me you met with her."

"Yes."

"I hope you don't mind that she gave me your number. She knows I want to help."

Hell, no, she didn't mind. She wished she'd had time to prepare for the conversation, though. He'd caught her off guard.

"What have you found out so far?" he asked.

She suppressed a snort. Did he think she was that stupid? "Nothing that the police don't already know. Somehow Jackie disappeared without a trace—with someone's help."

"No leads at all?"

"No, but I'll keep digging."

"Who else will you be talking to?"

"Other members of Jackie's family," Casey said, at the same time she realized that she hadn't asked Ellen about aunts, uncles, and other relatives. They might know something. "They probably don't know anything, but I like to cover all the bases."

"And you haven't uncovered any clues so far, eh?"

Nothing that amounted to a flashing arrow pointing to Jackie's location, and nothing she wanted to share. "No." For someone who wanted to help, Hargrave seemed more interested in the state of her investigation. "Do you mind answering a few questions?"

"Uh . . ."

"You said you wanted to help."

"Sure, sure. Fire away."

"Did the doctors tell you the cause for Jackie's initial discomfort?"

"Why would they tell me? I'm not family."

"No, but Ellen was distraught, and Sissy told me you went looking for the doctor at one point."

Silence, then, "I was in shock. One minute she has stomach cramps, the next they're saying she's in a coma. I wanted to find out more, for Ellen, but they weren't interested in talking to me. They were too busy trying to figure out what the hell happened."

"You didn't overhear them saying anything?"

"They wouldn't let me into the room. One of the nurses told me Jackie was unconscious and made it clear that I was in the way."

"Where did you go after that? Sissy doesn't remember seeing you again."

"I went back to the waiting area, but Sissy and Ellen were gone. So I left. The nurse was right, I was in the way. Sissy and Ellen didn't need me hovering. I had no clue where they were, anyway, or how long they'd be."

Something didn't add up. Sissy had sat in the waiting room for a while, only leaving when she'd figured Mike wasn't coming back. Mike made it sound as if he'd only left the waiting room for a few minutes. "So you went to check on Jackie, the nurse shooed you away, and when you got back to the waiting room, Sissy and Ellen weren't there."

"That's right."

"Was the party food tested?"

"What do you mean?"

"Jackie fell ill at a company party—with stomach cramps. I assume someone took a look at the food."

"Over a hundred people were at that reception, but Jackie was the only one with cramps. It had nothing to do with the food."

"I'll take that to mean that nobody investigated that angle."

Mike forcefully exhaled. "If there was something wrong with the food, we would have had an epidemic of stomach cramps on our hands. It wasn't the food. Do you think the food is tested every time someone goes to a party and gets sick?"

No, but most people didn't fall into a coma. He had a point, though. Since it was only one person . . . the health department would only be interested when a bunch of people had food poisoning, and the police when there was a reason to suspect foul play. Unfortunately, the foul play had taken place weeks later and could be unrelated to Jackie's cramps. "How were things going at work for Jackie?"

"Fine," Mike said flatly.

"I'm trying to get a complete picture of her life. Anything you can tell me will help. Was she having problems at work?"

"I can't talk about that."

"You said you wanted to help . . ."

"I do. But I don't see how Jackie's work could relate to her disappearance." His voice hardened. "That's what you're investigating, isn't it? Her disappearance. Not the party. Not her performance evaluations. No, you want to find out who the hell showed up at the hospital and took her away. I want to know that, too."

He sounded defensive—and sincere.

"Check her personal life," he suggested. "It has to be someone who knows her. Who else would remove her from the hospital?"

More importantly, why? And why keep Ellen in the dark? "Was she seeing anyone?"

"I wouldn't know about that. Jackie kept to herself."

Casey considered asking him about Jackie's visits to security, but decided against it. Based on her conversation with Sissy, she knew he was withholding information, but he could be doing so out of loyalty to Jackie. She inwardly sighed. Did Jackie's work have anything to do with her disappearance, or was that angle a waste of time? Either way, the reason for Jackie's trips to the security office might have involved Mike. She didn't want to antagonize him unless she knew for sure.

"So you've got nothing, eh?" Mike said, making Casey bristle.

She bit her tongue and took a deep breath. "I'm still in the early stages of my investigation. I'm gathering information."

"Well, if you find out anything useful, let me know. I want to help. Here's my number."

Casey scribbled it down. At least the conversation had yielded one piece of solid information, but the only real lead she had was Street's emails.

Chapter Seven

Yawning into her hand, Casey stopped outside the coffee shop and checked her watch again. Yep, it was just after seven, and she was already showered, dressed, and ready to hold a coherent conversation. Her stomach grumbled. Time for a coffee and Danish. She swung the door open.

When she spotted Emily behind the counter, she wanted to turn around and slink back outside. Would Emily remember her stupid remark in the van? *I might be the last person she wants to see.* If not for the case . . . Casey waited for a businessman to collect his morning coffee, and forced a smile.

Emily's eyes widened slightly. "I normally don't see you at this time."

"I was hoping to run into you."

Her brows shot up. "Really."

"Yeah," Casey said, wishing she could start over and say, "I require your expertise." She scratched her head. "I need to ask you something."

"Sure. What is it?"

She eyed the jogger who'd come into the shop behind her. "It's private. Maybe when you're on a break?"

Emily grimaced. "The morning rush is about to start. I'll be run off my feet until my shift is over."

Shit, she should have realized. "Sorry."

"No, don't be sorry. Can you come back around 8:30? We can chat then."

"Sure. And I'll have a coffee and two Danishes to go."

"Raspberry and strawberry, right?" Emily bagged the Danishes and poured a coffee. After accepting the loonies and toonies Casey fished from her pocket, she made change and handed everything to Casey. "See you at 8:30."

"See you then," Casey said, mentally kicking herself. She should have known that Emily's shift would be busy. If she'd thought it through, she could have called the shop last night and found out when Emily's morning shift ended. Her body would have appreciated another hour in bed.

One raspberry Danish, two coffees, and just over an hour later, she returned to the coffee shop and waited while Emily served a couple of customers. Emily disappeared into the back and returned without her apron and hair net. "This is for me," she said, pouring herself a coffee to go. "You want one?"

"No, thanks." One more coffee and they'd be scraping her off the ceiling.

"Let's go outside."

She trailed after Emily, squinting into the morning sun until Emily whirled and quirked a brow at her. "So what did you want to ask me . . . in private?"

Casey had the distinct impression that Emily was holding her breath. "Well, I was wondering if—"

Emily's phone rang. She groaned and glanced at its display. "Sorry, I have to take this. It's my sister-in-law. Hello?" Silence. "What thingie?" Emily sipped her coffee. "Is it plugged in? Okay, but what about the computer? Is it plugged into the computer?" She listened. "No! Don't plug it in there. Look for one that matches the—okay, good." She fell silent again. "Nothing? But you said it was working last night, right? Did you change anything, install any new software?" Another pause. "I don't know why it won't scan. It could be any number of reasons." She rolled her eyes at Casey. "Look, I have to go. Why don't you uninstall and reinstall the software, and if it still doesn't work, give me a call and I'll drop by later, okay? Bye." She snapped her phone shut and shook her head. "I hate that!"

"What?"

"That! Would you see a gynecologist for your heart?"

Was this a trick question? "Uh, no."

"Exactly. Because everyone's specialized, right? You don't see a cardiologist for foot problems. You don't see a family lawyer for murder."

Casey smiled and nodded.

"Just because I'm doing a computer degree, everyone calls me when they run into a technical problem. I study interpretive computer languages. I'm not a hardware person. I don't work on websites. I know diddly about networks. But someone's scanner isn't working and I'm expected to magically know how to fix it, because I'm in computers. Someone can't connect to the Internet—hey, call Emily. Tell Emily, 'My game keeps crashing,' and she'll instantly know how to solve the problem. Have a question about one of the thousands of software programs out there? Ask Emily!" She blew out a sigh. "Don't mind me. I only freak out at every fiftieth question. Anyway, where were we? You wanted to ask me something."

"Uh, yeah." Question number fifty-one, apparently. Forget about asking her to look at the emails. Casey would end up wearing Emily's coffee. She shifted her weight. "You know what? It's not important. Let's forget about it."

Emily smiled coyly. "Come on, don't chicken out now. You've come this far."

"No, it's okay."

Her face fell. She looked disappointed . . . *really* disappointed. What had she thought—wait a minute. Did Emily think . . . shit! She'd never dinged Casey's gaydar. Casey cleared her throat and stared at Emily. No, she must have it wrong. Even if they did bat for the same team, Emily wouldn't be interested, and she'd never turned Casey's crank either—mainly because Casey hadn't looked. Emily *was* kind of cute—and a freaking computer genius. No, this line of thought was nuts. She needed more sleep. Getting up at an ungodly hour had addled her mind. "I'm sorry, I shouldn't have bothered you."

"Don't worry about it," Emily mumbled. She pulled a key from her pocket and gestured toward a nearby sedan. "I have to go, or I'll be late for class. See you around, okay?" She turned away.

"Yeah, sure," Casey said, dismayed by Emily's flat tone and her haste to get to her car. She felt like a first class asshole. What harm would having a friendly meal with Emily do? The moment she told Emily what she did for a living—ha! Was *trying* to do for a living—Emily would wonder why the hell she'd ever been interested, and that was if Casey was reading the situation correctly. Emily could be as straight as an arrow. Maybe she'd thought . . . what? That Casey was going to hand her a wad of cash, or a winning lottery ticket, or tell her she'd won a new car? If she hadn't expected Casey to ask her out, then what else—

A car engine roared to life. Casey snapped out of it. "Emily!" She jumped up and down and flailed her arms in the air, then ran to the car and rapped on the driver's window. Emily lowered it and looked up at her. Casey swallowed. "Do you want to have dinner with me?"

A smile split Emily's face. "I'd love to have dinner with you."

"Really? I mean, sure. Okay. When is good for you?"

"Tomorrow night?"

"Sure. We could, well, there's that restaurant on, uh . . ." The street name eluded her frozen brain. God, why were the crinkles at the corners of Emily's eyes suddenly making her knees go weak?

"Why don't you meet me here at 6:30?" Emily said calmly. "I don't think we need to go anywhere swanky that requires a reservation."

Casey's wallet certainly didn't.

"We can decide tomorrow."

"Sure." Casey shoved her hands into her pockets. "Anyway, I won't keep you."

"Yeah, I should get to class. I'll be looking forward to tomorrow night."

"Me too," Casey said, knowing she had a silly grin on her face. She waved as Emily pulled out of the parking spot, and kept waving until she could no longer see the car. Shit! She didn't have Emily's phone number. What if something related to the case came up and Casey couldn't make it tomorrow? Why hadn't Emily asked for her phone number? What if she turned out to be another Leah and blabbed on about herself all night? What if it was another audition? What if Emily was laughing right now about the big joke she'd just played on the idiot who thought they'd be going on a date?

Okay, first, why would Emily play a cruel prank on one of the coffee shop's customers? Second, why was Casey freaking out about tomorrow's dinner not being real, or not being able to make it, when having dinner hadn't been on her radar five minutes ago? Third, why couldn't she stop smiling?

When she unlocked her apartment door and stepped into the hallway, she thought she'd got the grinning under control, but the moment she saw Gran, she smiled again.

Gran looked up from buttering her toast. "You look pleased with yourself."

"I think I'm going on a date tomorrow."

"What?"

Casey sighed and moved closer to the table. "I think I'm going out on a date tomorrow," she said loudly.

"You think?"

"You know Emily at the coffee shop?"

Gran nodded and bit into her toast.

"I just asked her to have dinner with me tomorrow, but I'm not sure it's a date. I might have misread everything."

Nodding, Gran chewed furiously, then swallowed. "It's a date," she said.

Casey folded her arms. "How do you know?"

"I told her you're a lesbian."

"What?" Casey shrieked. "Why? When?"

"You forgot who and where."

"I already know the answers to those." Casey pulled out a chair and plunked into it. "Why the hell would you tell her I'm a lesbian?"

"Because every time I see her, she asks about you. I'm not slow, you know." Gran raised her eyebrows. "You are, though."

As opposed to Gran, who sometimes took an early morning walk, Casey had rarely crossed paths with Emily since she'd switched to the morning shift. "Jesus, Gran, you could have told me. How did you slip it into the conversation? You didn't just bluntly put it out there, did you?" She imagined Emily asking what Gran would like to order, and Gran responding, "Casey's a lesbian." "Please tell me you subtly worked it into a conversation when it made sense."

Gran's face tightened. "Give me some credit, for Christ's sake." She took another bite of her toast and slowly chewed it.

Knowing Gran was intentionally trying to irritate her, Casey tried not to fidget, but finally blurted, "Come on, tell me!"

"You young people have no patience," Gran grumbled. "A few months ago—"

"A few months? She's known for a few months?"

"She asked whether you had a boyfriend. I said, no, she's a lesbian. Is that acceptable to you?"

"Did she ask if I had a girlfriend?"

Gran shook her head. "I told her you haven't had one for ages, though."

"Well, thank you. Thank you very much!"

"What? It's the truth."

An embarrassing truth.

"It didn't stop her from agreeing to have dinner with you," Gran said, her eyes on Casey's face.

"I suppose so," Casey mumbled.

"You'll thank me at the wedding."

"Wedding! We're going out for dinner." And she wasn't sure how she felt about Emily. Surprise was fuelling her anticipation, more than anything. It wasn't love at first sight; it was more "Emily seems pleasant, so why not?"

"That's what I said when I first started dating your grandfather. It's only dinner. And now look. That dinner led to you sitting on that chair." Gran waved her half-eaten piece of toast at Casey. "Emily's a nice girl. You always choose losers."

"Excuse me?"

"It's true. They're always shallow and stick around for five minutes."

Casey bit her tongue. She couldn't lash out when Gran was right.

"I've been putting in a good word with someone decent, and it's finally paid off. Don't screw it up."

Casey wanted to groan. How many lesbians went on dates arranged by their grandmothers? "I'm not hearing violins."

"Give it a chance," Gran bellowed. "You could do worse than having a good friendship as the foundation. You don't believe those movies where they're still swinging from the chandelier after being married for twenty years, do you? I thought you kids were supposed to be jaded. When the honeymoon ends, you'd better like whoever you're stuck with."

"Jesus, Gran, why don't you trample over the rest of my dreams while you're at it."

Gran tutted. "Stop getting ahead of yourself. You're going on a date. You're not getting married."

It took all of Casey's willpower to not snatch the other piece of toast from Gran's plate and throw it at her.

CASEY WINCED WHEN Ellen answered her phone and said, "I won't ask if you have anything to report."

"I'm working on a lead."

"You are," Ellen breathed. "What?"

"Let me work it first. If it pans out, I'll tell you. I'm calling to find out about your mother's other relatives. Siblings, cousins, anyone she might confide in."

Ellen snorted. "I was hoping you wouldn't need to talk to Aunt Joan."

"Why?"

"She's a bit of an odd duck. Mom saw her at least once a month. Oh, shit." Ellen fell silent for a moment. "I'm talking about her in the past tense. Shit."

Not knowing what to say, Casey waited for Ellen to collect herself.

"What was I saying?" Ellen finally said in a more subdued tone.

"Aunt Joan."

"Right. I don't know how close they were—are, but Mom saw her regularly. As to whether she told her anything . . . who knows? Do you have to talk to her? She can be . . . trying."

"What if she knows something that can lead us to your mother?"

"Oh, fiddlesticks." Ellen blew out some air. "Do I have to go with you?"

Cripes, what was it with Aunt Joan? Casey wanted to lie and say yes, but Ellen had enough on her mind already. "Only if you think your being there will help."

"I suppose I can go with you." Ellen sounded as if she'd be more enthusiastic about undergoing surgery in prehistoric times. "I'll call her, set up a time. Saturday?"

"Can you make it Sunday? I'm going to a cat show on Saturday. I'm seeing someone there about your mother." Hey, she was working two leads, not one, though she hadn't figured out her next step regarding

Street's emails. She wanted to ask Emily about them, but she didn't want to ruin their date.

"I'll try for Sunday afternoon."

"Doesn't she call you to find out if there's any news about your mother?"

Ellen chuckled. "She emails me once a week. I haven't mentioned you to her, though. I guess I'll have to now."

"You don't want her to know that you hired an investigator?"

"Her emails are rants, first about the hospital, then about me, then about the police. Everyone's incompetent. If she was in charge, Mom would be home. In fact, she never would have stayed in the hospital in the first place, because Aunt Joan would have diagnosed the problem and taken care of it before Mom slipped into a coma. You'll just be another thing to rant about." Ellen paused. "Hopefully she won't do it to your face."

Great. A cat show on Saturday, and an armchair investigator on Sunday. But first, her dinner with Emily.

Chapter Eight

CASEY SLIPPED ANOTHER piece of pizza onto her plate and took a sip of water. Apart from having pizza yet again—thank god she loved the stuff—so far, so good. Emily had shown up on time, and the drive to a nearby family restaurant hadn't been awkward. Casey felt more at home in this casual atmosphere than she had in the swanky restaurant with Leah. Jeans and a blouse were more her style than dress pants and a matching jacket. The desire to impress wasn't driving her, either. She didn't want to make an ass of herself, but the pressure to sound brilliant wasn't there.

"So what do you do?" Emily asked.

Casey tensed. Okay, what she'd just said to herself about not needing to impress? Not entirely true, but her discomfort with the dreaded question wasn't specific to Emily. Being so new at the game, calling herself a private investigator didn't sit right. Maybe when she had a solved case or two under her belt . . . She wiped her mouth with a napkin, then said, "I'm a private investigator."

Emily stared at her. "Really?"

"I'm new. I—I'm working my first case. I—"

Emily held up her hand. "I'm surprised, that's all. It's not the answer I expected. Why a private investigator? I thought you were working at Walmart."

Casey felt her face flush. God, how embarrassing. Why the hell was someone who was working on her PhD sitting having pizza with a former Walmart minion pretending to be a private investigator? "I was. But I always saw that as temporary." That was what she'd told herself when she'd graduated from high school with no burning desire to be anything. Most of her friends had applied to university and looked forward to taking the next step on the path to their dream careers. She'd trudged from store to fast food joint, dropping off a resume that listed the glamorous skills she'd acquired from her summer jobs serving behind counters at food courts. "I didn't know what I wanted to do when I left high school."

"So why a private investigator?" Emily asked again.

"I'd helped a few people find their missing pets. One of them said I had a knack and should be a pet detective, like Ace Ventura." It sounded so stupid now. She couldn't believe she'd seen it as a sign from the Universe—and that she was telling Emily about it. "It got me thinking. I figured limiting myself to pets would be dumb." When Emily grinned, Casey couldn't tell whether she thought the *entire* notion of being an investigator was dumb. "Either way, I needed an investigator's licence, so I got one."

"I'm sure it wasn't as easy as that." Emily lifted a piece of pizza from the platter and bit into it.

"I had to take an exam. I took courses at a security college."

Emily swallowed her mouthful of pizza. "Working and going to school can be rough. It takes dedication."

Casey's modesty wouldn't allow her to nod. "What about you?" she said, wanting to shift the focus away from herself. "How did you end up where you are?"

"It's not where I expected to be, that's for sure."

"How could you end up doing a PhD without any planning?" Casey blurted.

Emily's answering smile sent a surge of warmth through Casey. "I was working on my Bachelor of Arts in sociology when I decided to take a computer course. Grudgingly, I might add. I had to choose from a list of electives, and the other courses didn't interest me at all. So I held my nose and hoped the programming course wouldn't be too difficult or boring."

"You liked it."

"To put it mildly. Nobody was more surprised than me. I switched majors, went on to graduate school, and here I am."

"What about sociology?"

Emily shrugged. "I thought it was what I wanted to do, and it still interests me. But the fire just wasn't there, not like it is for interpretive languages."

"I'm not sure I should ask what that is, because I probably won't understand the answer."

"I'm sure I could explain it to you, but I'd rather find out more about what you do." Emily pushed her plate away. "You said you're working on a case?"

"Yeah."

"Can you tell me about it, or is it top secret? How'd you get it? Do you have an office?"

Casey chuckled. "No. I don't even have business cards," she said before she could stop herself.

Emily's eyes danced. "You should definitely get business cards."

"Yeah, I'm planning to. As for the case . . . I can only speak in generalities. It's a missing person case. One of my friends recommended me to someone."

"Good friend," Emily murmured. "How's the case going?"

"I'm working a couple of leads." Casey swallowed. She couldn't let this opportunity go by. "Do you know anything about email?"

"I take it you mean beyond how to send and receive it?" Emily said dryly.

"Yeah. I know you said you hate it when people assume you know everything about anything related to computers, but . . . one of my leads is a bunch of emails. I'm just wondering if I could somehow find the sender."

Emily frowned. "It would be a long shot. The IP address would have to be tied to one person."

The what?

"Finding out who that person is will be next to impossible. It's the sort of thing the police need a warrant for, otherwise ISPs won't release that information."

The who?

"If you have the IP address, you can usually find out what city the person is in, though."

"I don't suppose . . ."

"You want me to do it." Emily blinked at her. "Wait. This is what you wanted to ask me when you came to the shop, isn't it?"

"Uh—"

"And I railroaded you into dinner. Oh, god." She picked up her napkin and held it against her mouth.

Aghast, Casey wanted to reach out and touch Emily's arm, but she didn't move. "No! I mean, okay, yeah, that's what I wanted to ask, but I wouldn't have asked you to dinner if I didn't want to have dinner with you." Her mortification deepened when Emily didn't respond. "I'm serious. I'm glad we're having dinner together. I'm enjoying it. I'm hoping we'll go to a movie or a club afterward." She realized it was true as she said it. "Emily, you were leaving. I stopped you to ask you to dinner."

Emily's eyes met Casey's. "You have those emails . . ."

"No. That's not why I stopped you. I stopped you because I twigged that you were gay, which hadn't even entered my mind before that point. I wanted to have dinner with you."

"You didn't know I'm gay?" Emily said, lowering the napkin.

"No."

"I thought you knew." She shook her head. "How stupid! I thought your grandmother was dropping hints about you because you were interested in me."

It was more that Gran had been interested in getting them together, and Casey suddenly understood why Gran hadn't told her about Emily. It would have smacked of matchmaking and instantly turned Casey off the idea of ever dating her. "Look, can we forget about the emails, because that's honestly not why I'm here. I shouldn't have mentioned them."

"I asked you about the case," Emily pointed out, making Casey feel worse. Emily shouldn't be defending her!

"True, but I didn't have to bring them up." Funny how she'd had a somewhat cavalier attitude to this evening—no violins!—but now desperately hoped she hadn't blown it. The soaring violins still weren't there, but she had the feeling that a song could break out at any time. Not wanting to fidget, she reached for her napkin and patted her mouth as she waited for Emily to say something. The silence stretched on. *Shit.*

"Did you mean it when you said you want to go out after this?" Emily finally said.

If Emily was setting Casey up to tell her to go to hell, she deserved it. "Yeah, I did. And you know, maybe I'm glad the email thing came out, because if we're going to start something . . . get to know each other . . . I guess it's better you find out now that I'm a bumbling idiot."

Emily's mouth twitched. "Save the emails to a thumb drive and drop it off at the shop."

"You don't have to," Casey said.

"I doubt I'll be able to help, but I'll have a look."

"Thanks." But she felt dismayed. Emily hadn't confirmed that they were starting something. Gran would be disappointed.

The waitress stopped at their table and started to collect their dishes. "Coffee?"

Casey looked to Emily, who nodded and said, "Please."

Casey's spirits lifted. "I'll have one too, please."

When the waitress left, Emily leaned back in her chair. "I think I'd prefer a movie over a club, if that's okay."

Casey struggled to not leap out of her chair and thrust her fist into the air. "Yeah. Absolutely. We can check what's playing around here."

"As for getting to know each other better . . . I'd like that." Emily folded her arms. "But I want to take things slow, okay? Not because of the emails. I just . . ." Her voice dwindled.

Casey could tell she was flailing. "Slow suits me just fine." Heck, she was ecstatic that Emily didn't hate her. She was also curious about the reason behind Emily's caution, but wouldn't pry. Maybe Emily wasn't long out of her last relationship, or maybe Casey was on probation. Time to move on before awkwardness set in. "What types of movies do you like?"

AS CASEY RODE the bus to the cat show, she reflected on her date with Emily the previous evening. They'd enjoyed the movie, and the drive home had been a comfortable one. Emily had dropped Casey off in front of her building. No kiss. Taking it slow. They hadn't arranged another date, but Emily had texted her that morning and said she'd enjoyed herself and would call her. Yep, they'd exchanged phone numbers, at least, and Casey expected that Emily *would* call.

She wouldn't give out her phone number and then use the "Don't call me, I'll call you" routine, right?

A jab on her leg broke her out of her reverie. "How many more stops?" Gran asked.

Casey peered out the window to get her bearings. "We're around five minutes away."

Gran grunted. "You should have asked Emily to come with you."

"We only just saw each other last night." Casey turned to her. "We're taking things slow."

"Oh." Gran's tone spoke volumes.

"We're not blowing each other off. We'll be seeing each other again. She already texted me this morning."

Gran's brows lifted. "So it went okay, then."

"Yeah." Though a couple of doubts had crept in, more to do with Casey's insecurities. What if they eventually got serious? Would Casey get along with Emily's friends? They were probably all geniuses. "She's twenty-six," she said, voicing another concern.

"So? She's only three years older than you."

"She's working on her PhD."

"That sounds good to me." Gran's eyes narrowed. "Stop looking for excuses to not see her. If you don't want to see her, don't see her."

"I *do* want to see her."

"Well, then?"

It was more that Casey couldn't believe Emily was interested in her. Usually Casey was the one with the crush, the one who'd suffered in silence for months, admiring from afar. Yes, she'd asked Emily out, but on a whim. She hadn't hung around the coffee shop hoping to snatch a few minutes of conversation with her, hadn't lain on her bed daydreaming about their perfect life together. Emily hadn't been on her radar, but apparently she'd been on Emily's. She couldn't shake the feeling that as Emily got to know her, she'd realize that she'd made a terrible mistake.

"Remember, when we find the person I'm looking for, let me do the talking," Casey said, wanting to think about something else.

Gran huffed. "I won't have anything to say. I'm not even sure why they have cat shows. Dogs do things. They chase balls, do tricks, sit, heel. Cats don't do anything except ignore you and eat plants."

"Mid keeps us company."

"Especially when she wants something."

Gran's attitude didn't fool Casey. One of them spoiled Mid rotten, and it wasn't her. "I think cat shows are all about how closely a cat matches its breed standard." At least that was what she'd learned when she'd done a quick search.

Gran sniffed. "Sounds boring to me."

"Keep that opinion to yourself, okay?" Casey said, imagining a riot breaking out over a flippant comment from Gran. "These people are serious about their breeds."

"Don't worry, I won't tell anyone what I really think."

That would be a first. "I'm sure there will be vendors there. You might find something for Mid."

"Ooh," Gran said, brightening. Yep, Mid had her wrapped around her little paw.

An hour later, Casey had to admit that Gran was on her best behaviour. When they'd stood and watched a judge examine a cat, lifting it, stretching it out, and waving around a feather, Gran's tongue must have bled. Now they were watching a similar display with a different breed. Gran didn't say a word, but she shook her head as they walked away. "Don't get it," she muttered. "Now, where can I get something for Mid? And when are you going to talk to that person so we can go home?"

Casey sighed. "I saw a sign back there pointing to the vendor room. As for Donna Wilkins, according to this," she held up the program book they'd bought on the way in, "she's over in Hall B."

"What the hell are we doing standing around watching cats for, then?"

"I don't want it to be obvious that I'm only here to talk to Wilkins."

Gran snorted. "Nobody's taking a blind bit of notice of us two." Her face softened when Casey scowled. "But I suppose it doesn't hurt to put on appearances, and you have."

"I guess I can talk to Wilkins now," Casey admitted. "Come on." She'd imposed on Gran enough. The cat show obviously wasn't enthralling her, but Gran had pretended to be interested and quietly endured. If she splurged on Mid, Casey wouldn't tease her about it.

They stopped inside the entrance to Hall B while Casey examined the floor map. "Wilkins should be just over here," she murmured, walking that way. "Now, let me do the talking."

"What are you going to say?"

"I'm going to somehow get on the topic of cat food, mention their brand, and hope she starts talking about work." Yeah, lame, and Gran's expression made it clear that she agreed. "If that doesn't work, I'll mention knowing Sissy."

"Why don't you tell her the truth?"

"Because she might not talk to me."

"She might be more willing to talk to you. Why would she tell a stranger work secrets for no reason?"

"Supposedly she's a gossip." But maybe Gran was right and honesty would be the best policy. If Casey's attempts to get Wilkins to open up failed, admitting that she'd hadn't run into her accidentally wouldn't engender trust. "I'll see how she comes across to me. If—"

"What the hell is that?" Gran bellowed, drawing looks.

Casey followed her gaze, then hurried after her when Gran marched up to the two women glaring at her.

"This, Madam, is a Sphynx," one of the women said, her nostrils flaring. "This is my cat, Felda."

Casey studied the hairless cat standing on the metal table, and resisted whacking Gran across the head with the program. One of these two women was probably Donna Wilkins.

"It doesn't have any fur," Gran said, stating the obvious.

"Of course *she* doesn't."

"Actually, she's not completely hairless," said the other woman.

"I don't see any fur," Gran said. "What the hell is the point of a cat without fur? Cats purr and have fur. It's what makes them cute. A cat without fur is like a porcupine without quills, or a beaver without teeth."

"A giraffe with no neck. A camel without humps," the other woman offered. She winced when Felda's owner whirled toward her. "Sorry," she mumbled.

"You've heard of hairless cats," Casey said to Gran, hoping to calm the situation.

"Hearing about something and actually seeing it are two different things. I said as much to your grandfather on our wedding night," she said out of the side of her mouth to Casey.

"Aw, Gran!" Jesus, she could do without the mental image Gran's words had conjured.

"What? I'd never seen the penthouse suite at the hotel before. When one of my friends described it to me—she spent her wedding night there, too—I thought she was exaggerating. Gold-plated toilet seat, my ass. But it was true." A smile played across Gran's lips. "What did you think I meant?"

Casey pressed her lips together and shook her head.

Gran turned back to the cat. "Most of us want to hide our wrinkles. Now I understand why some people think they've seen aliens. If I saw this in the house, I'd call the police."

"Gran!" Casey barked. The cat blinked at her.

"It's all right," said Felda's owner, but her thin lips and tight face said otherwise. "I see times like this as an opportunity to educate. The Sphynx originated not far from here, you know. In Toronto."

"A cat with no fur in our winters? Whose brilliant idea was that?" Gran asked, making Casey cringe.

"They don't go outside," the other woman said.

"What's their temperament like?" Casey asked. Shifting their attention to her wouldn't help, but she'd try anyway.

Felda's owner almost smiled. "They're very extroverted and affectionate."

"They're also highly intelligent," her companion said.

Gran's brow furrowed. "The cat doesn't have any fur and lives in Ontario. How intelligent can it be?"

Casey wanted to cry. It was too late to pretend that she and Gran didn't know each other.

"Can I touch it?" Gran asked.

"No," its owner said immediately.

"Oh, come on, Donna. Let her stroke Felda," the other woman said.

Donna? Casey inwardly groaned.

"She might pass on germs," Donna said.

Gran's eyes bulged. "I beg your pardon?"

"Don't take it personally. I don't let anyone touch Felda at these shows."

When Gran drew breath, Casey quickly stepped in. "Why don't you go to the vendor's hall?" she suggested, figuring her chances of talking to Donna might climb to 0.000001 percent if Gran wasn't nearby. "I'll meet you there."

Gran frowned. "I don't even know where it is."

"Here." Casey tapped the map page in the program, then thrust it toward Gran. "It's near the entrance."

"Why don't I take you over there," said Donna's companion. "I want to get some air."

As Casey silently thanked the woman, Donna tutted and shook her head. Casey nudged Gran's arm. "Go with her. I won't be long." Especially since she suspected her conversation with Donna would consist of Donna telling her to f-off.

"This way," Donna's companion said, taking Gran's elbow.

Gran slapped her hand away. "I can walk on my own!" she snapped.

Casey could see Gran's head moving as they strolled away. The poor woman with her was getting an earful, but about what? Hairless cats? Gran's opinion of the cat show? The sitcom she'd watched last night? When Casey turned back toward Donna, she froze. The cat was gone, along with Donna. She let out her pent breath when she spotted Donna putting Felda into a nearby cage.

"What a horrible experience for you," Casey heard Donna say as she approached her. "Don't pay any attention, Fel. They're ignorant, all of them." Felda's eyes closed when Donna stroked her under her chin. Okay, so Felda sort of looked cute right now. Casey wouldn't deliberately go out and get a hairless cat, but if one was in trouble or needed a home, she wouldn't turn it away. Neither would Gran.

"Oh, my little Fel-fel," Donna cooed.

Casey cleared her throat. Donna looked over her shoulder. Her voice hardened. "Oh. You're still here."

"Yeah," Casey said, throwing out Plans A and B, which would be useless now. "You're Donna Wilkins, right?"

Donna closed the cage door. "That's right." She peered curiously at Casey.

"I was hoping to run into you here. I'm looking into Jackie Rose's disappearance. Someone said you might be able to give me the rundown on the office politics in her department."

"You working for the hospital?"

"No, her daughter."

Donna's eyes bored into Casey. "If I wasn't so fond of Jackie, I'd tell you to shove off."

"I'd understand why. Sorry about my grandmother."

"Your grandmother, eh?" Donna smirked. "Don't take this the wrong way, but you have my sympathies."

Casey's back went up. In exactly what way was she supposed to take it? But she held her temper. After the disaster with Gran, she couldn't blame Donna for wanting to take a shot at her. Gran had insulted Donna's cat, for god's sake.

"Who told you to talk to me?"

Casey hesitated. "I'd rather not reveal my source. I'll just say it's someone who doesn't work for the company anymore."

Donna pursed her lips. If she suspected Kenny, she wasn't saying. "I don't know what to tell you."

"You said you're fond of Jackie. Were you friends?" Casey had the impression that Sissy was Jackie's only work confidante.

"No, but she never caused problems. Never made trivial demands. Came in every day and did her job, which is more than I can say about some others in my departments."

"I've heard that there might have been problems in Jackie's department. I know you're under a strict confidentiality agreement—"

Donna waved a dismissive hand. "Our competitors don't care about who doesn't get along with whom." Her brows knitted. "Do you think Jackie's disappearance has something to do with work?"

"I don't know," Casey said levelly. "I'm trying to gather as much information as I can." She could see that her response hadn't stopped Donna's wheels from turning.

"For Jackie," Donna murmured with a sigh. "Mike is going nuts, because Jackie is his top scientist and he's under the gun to produce a new formula right now. This might sound horrible, but it's amusing to see him make it appear that he's freaking out because he's concerned about her well-being, when we all know things weren't great between them and he's really upset because his job is on the line, along with everyone else's in his department."

"It's that bad?"

Donna gave Casey an indulgent look. "This is a cut-throat business. We're neck and neck with our closest competitor, and we haven't brought out anything new in almost a year. I'm under a lot of pressure to produce a meal that Fluffy will devour, and that means my employees are under the gun too, especially Mike. Feline nutrition is his baby. If he doesn't come through, he's history. And let's just say . . . no, I shouldn't tell you that."

"What?"

Donna shook her head. "I can't."

Casey struggled to restrain her frustration. "Donna, you said you want to help Jackie. If there's anything you know . . . if you think Mike might have something to do with her disappearance—"

"No. Quite the opposite, in fact." Donna moistened her lips. "Without Jackie, I doubt Mike's team will meet their deadline. Jackie was the lynchpin, for everyone. The last thing Mike would have wanted was for her to disappear. The coma was bad enough. I think he called the hospital five times a day to see if there were any signs that she was coming out of it."

A thought sprang into Casey's mind: maybe he wanted to make sure she *wasn't* coming out of it. That possibility ran counter to Donna's belief that Jackie's presence at work was invaluable to Mike, but ever since the meeting with Sissy, Casey's gut had told her that Mike had something to do with Jackie's stomach cramps. Now she wondered if her instincts were leading her astray. Mike's insistence that he drive Jackie and Sissy to the hospital had aroused her suspicions, but he might have wanted to ensure that his top scientist received the best care possible. "Have you replaced Jackie with anyone?"

Donna frowned. "Replaced?"

Bad word choice.

"Mike hired a junior scientist to round out the team, but everyone knows it's temporary—at least, we hope it is. We want Jackie back. Does that sound naïve, that we still expect her back?"

Maybe. "No."

"What could have happened? Who would take her away?"

"What do you think happened?"

Donna's eyes widened. "I don't know. The most popular theory seems to be that someone who cares about her wasn't satisfied with her treatment and moved her to another clinic. But why the secrecy? Why not tell her daughter?" She lowered her voice. "Do you think we're kidding ourselves? She's not coming back, is she?"

"I wouldn't lose hope yet." Casey was determined to find Jackie—hopefully alive. "Who's in charge now—among the scientists, I mean?"

"One of the other senior scientists who worked closely with Jackie. But he doesn't have Jackie's initiative. She drove everything in that department. They're building on what she started. Whether they'll produce a worthy formula, and on time, remains to be seen."

"When did you hire the new scientist? After Jackie disappeared?"

"No, a couple of weeks after she went into the coma, when it became clear that she wasn't going to be on her feet anytime soon. Even if she had come around, she'd have needed time to recover. Mike came to me and said he'd definitely miss the deadline with one person down, so I approved the hire."

"And he did the hiring?"

Donna nodded. "It *is* his department. He would have had at least one of the scientists interview the prospects, though. I haven't had any complaints about the new guy."

"What's his name?"

"I can't tell you that," Donna said. "Sorry."

"Anything else you can tell me that you think might help?"

"No. Jackie was a model employee. Why would anyone want to kidnap her? That's the real mystery, isn't it?"

Yes, it was. The why would lead to the who, but Casey was more confused now than she had been before speaking with Donna. Was Mike a good guy or bad guy? Did Jackie's disappearance have anything to do with work, or had she hidden a part of her life from her daughter? Heck, was Jackie a random victim? Who would want a comatose woman? Medical researchers? Satanic worshippers? Some sick psychopath? But what about the handwriting on the power of attorney? It had to be someone who knew Jackie, or at least had access to a handwriting sample. "Thanks for talking with me," Casey said. "Especially after my grandmother."

"Do you have a cat?" Donna asked.

"Yeah, but she's not a pedigree."

Donna's mouth pinched. "I see."

Casey could hear the sniff.

"NOW, DON'T TAKE anything she says personally," Ellen said nervously as she led Casey up the path to Jackie's sister's house. "When she runs off at the mouth, we just nod and smile." She hovered her finger over the doorbell. "Ready?"

"Ready," Casey said, not sure what to expect.

Ellen rang the doorbell, and put on a strained smile when the door swung open. "Aunt Joan," she said.

Joan squinted at them. "You'd better come in."

The moment Casey stepped into the house, the stench of stale cigarette smoke assaulted her nostrils. In the living room, an overflowing ashtray sat on every available surface, including the end table next to what was obviously Joan's favourite chair. An open pack of cigarettes and a lighter were also within arm's reach.

"Sit down," Joan growled, plunking into her own chair. She waited until Casey and Ellen had settled onto the sofa, then said, "I don't know anything."

"Then why did you agree to meet with Casey?" Ellen asked, failing to keep the exasperation out of her voice.

"Because I wanted to see who you'd hired." She slid a cigarette from the packet, lit up, and took a long drag. "All I can say is, God help us. Or, rather, God help Jackie." Joan blew smoke in Casey's direction. "How old are you? Twelve?"

Ellen gasped. "Aunt Joan!"

"You must be getting desperate."

Casey's hands clenched. Nod and smile. Grin and bear it.

"Casey's already found out that the spa weekend contest was a sham, which is more than the police did," Ellen said.

Joan scoffed. "I figured that out myself, ages ago."

"You did not!"

"Did too."

"Why didn't you say anything, then?" Ellen snapped.

"I wanted to see if any of the idiots would figure it out."

"No, it's because you didn't figure it out."

"What do you think?" Joan said to Casey.

Nope. She wasn't falling into that trap.

"If you suspected the contest was a sham, you would have told the police," Ellen said. "You want to find Mom as much as I do."

"Have *you* told the police?" Joan looked at Casey.

Ellen drew breath.

"I'm talking to your sidekick," Joan bellowed. "Is she mute? She hasn't said a word since she came in."

Wishing she could leave, since Joan apparently couldn't help, Casey forced herself to answer. "Yes, I told the police. They noted the information."

"Ha! Noted the information." Joan took another drag of her cigarette. "Idiots, all of them. They're not looking for your mom, Ellen. If the solution doesn't drop out of the sky and whack them on the head, they move on. That's why I didn't tell them about the contest. What would have been the point?"

"Oh, please." Ellen let out a long, heartfelt sigh. "Did Mom say anything to you, or not?"

Joan waved her cigarette at Casey. "I thought she would be asking the questions."

"Did Jackie seem upset about anything before the night she fell into a coma?" Casey asked, doing her best to sound as if she were interested.

"Nope."

"Did she say anything that sounded strange to you?"

Joan cackled. "You haven't met Jackie, have you? Jackie always sounds strange."

"No, she did—doesn't." Ellen folded her arms.

"Anything that set off alarm bells, I mean, or made you wonder," Casey said.

Joan flicked a lengthy piece of ash from her cigarette into the ashtray. "Nope."

"Do you have any theories about what might have happened to her?"

"Oh god," Ellen murmured.

Joan's eyes narrowed. "Of course I do. Do you want to hear what I think?"

Casey braced herself. "Yes."

"She has a secret lover. She didn't want this one to know," she cocked her head toward Ellen, "because she didn't want to upset her. Ellen's excitable."

"No, I'm not! I'm not excitable!" Ellen shrieked. "Jesus, Mom's missing, and all you can do is take shots at me. Do you understand the hell I'm going through? Where were you when she was in hospital? Did you visit? What are you doing to find Mom? Secret lover? Bullshit. Mom has never hidden any boyfriends from me."

Joan appeared unfazed by Ellen's outburst. "You wouldn't know if she had, Ellen. Think about it."

"What do you mean? But—" Ellen's forehead furrowed.

"Why would a lover take her from the hospital, especially without consulting Ellen?" Casey asked.

Joan shrugged. "How the hell should I know? All I can say is this: according to the idiots, he had a legitimate power of attorney. He knew she was in the hospital. He knew this one would jump at a free spa weekend. She's always gone on and on and on about how she'd love to be pampered at a spa, but doesn't have the money."

Really? Casey mentally stored away that interesting tidbit.

"It's someone who knows Jackie, right? Isn't that obvious, or am I really the only one who isn't an idiot?" Joan took a final puff of her cigarette, squished the stub into the ashtray, and pulled another cigarette from the packet. "That's why I'm not too worried. Wherever she is, she's safe. Christ, if someone wanted to hurt her, a little injection into her IV would have done the trick. He wouldn't have gone through the trouble of kidnapping her."

"Then why kidnap her?" Casey asked, as she ran through the possibilities. Had he been dissatisfied with the hospital's handling of Jackie's case? Had he wanted Jackie to be treated at a specific clinic, maybe out of the country? Did he live in another province and he wanted Jackie closer to him? Why had he kept Ellen out of the picture?

"Forget all the crap about the spa and the food poisoning. Find him and you'll find her."

Casey bit her tongue. Thank you, Ms. Obvious, but easier said than done. Regardless of whether Steve Rose was friend or foe, he was the key to the case. "Steve Rose, the one who took her from the hospital . . . he claimed to be her son."

"And you're wondering if there are any family skeletons this one doesn't know about." Joan took several puffs of her cigarette, stretching the suspenseful silence. "Nope."

"No son."

"Nope. Just this one."

"And Mom and I are close. Real close," Ellen said. "She wouldn't keep a relationship from me, especially a serious one. Why would she do that, eh? Why, Aunt Joan?"

"You'll have to ask her," Joan said.

Ellen's face tightened. "There's no point asking her because she wouldn't keep it from me."

They glared at each other. Not expecting to learn anything useful from Joan, Casey interjected, "Well, thanks for seeing me. I don't have any more questions."

Joan's brows shot up. "That's it? I didn't tell you anything."

Not entirely true, and the visit had strengthened Casey's suspicion that Jackie knew Steve Rose. "Do you know anything that might help? If you know of a question I should have asked . . ." she said, appealing to Joan's ego.

"Nope."

Okay, then. She stood, wanting to avoid more bickering between Ellen and Joan.

"You don't mind seeing yourselves out, do you?" Joan said.

"No." Ellen started to follow Casey into the hallway, then changed her mind and walked back to Joan. "We should have dinner soon, okay?" She pecked Joan on the cheek. "I'll call you."

Outside, Ellen sniffed her jacket sleeve and groaned. "I'll have to throw everything into the laundry." She touched Casey's arm. "I'm sorry about that. I told you she can be difficult."

"It's okay," Casey mumbled.

"She's all I have now." Ellen blinked. "If we don't find Mom . . ."

"We'll find her."

Ellen nodded, but Casey didn't blame her for having doubts. They climbed into Ellen's car. Before firing up the engine, Ellen turned to her. "I must owe you more money by now."

"Yeah, but . . ." She felt guilty about taking more of Ellen's money when she hadn't made any real progress. Yes, she still had a lead—the emails—but if that didn't pan out, she had no idea what she'd do next.

"Work out how much and I'll write you a cheque when I drop you off," Ellen said. "Don't short-change yourself. You're the only one who's working on this, and I know you want to find Mom as much as I do."

True, but for different reasons. If Casey didn't find Jackie, she'd want to refund all of Ellen's money and never take another case. Maybe she wasn't cut out for this game.

Twenty minutes later, she let herself into the apartment and stared at the cheque in her hand. She'd better earn this money.

"Where the hell have you been?" Gran shouted from the sofa. "I've been trying to call you. We need bread."

Shit, she'd forgotten to turn her phone back on after leaving Joan's. "I'll nip out and get a loaf."

As she waited for the elevator, she pulled out her phone to check messages, and smiled when she listened to the one from Emily. Yes, she definitely wanted to meet to discuss the emails; in fact, she couldn't wait.

Chapter Nine

NOT WANTING TO give Emily the impression that she cared mostly about the emails, Casey was waiting for Emily to raise the subject. She lifted her hamburger and said, "Do you eat here often?" As soon as the words were out of her mouth, she wanted to groan at what sounded like a lame pickup line.

"It's close to the computer building." Emily sprinkled more salt on her fries. "Clean, fast, food is decent . . . I usually bring in my lunch. But when we go out, we usually come here. I occasionally meet friends here for dinner, too."

Did that include Casey? She wasn't sure if she was a friend, a girlfriend, or in a transitional stage between the two.

"By 'we,' I mean the graduate students, especially the ones studying under the same prof."

"I see," Casey said, not really seeing. Beyond knowing that students had to present a thesis, studying for a PhD was a mystery to her. What was she doing here? Emily wouldn't stay interested in a high school graduate pretending to be a private investigator for long.

Emily swallowed a mouthful of food and set her half-eaten hamburger on her plate. "About the emails . . ."

Casey casually sipped her Coke.

"I didn't find anything useful," Emily said with an apologetic smile. "All I can tell you is that whoever sent them used an ISP in Toronto. I'm sorry."

"Don't be sorry. You said you probably wouldn't find anything." Yet Emily had wanted to deliver the news in person—or maybe just wanted to have dinner with her but was afraid to ask. Either explanation was endearing.

"Do you have any other leads?" Emily asked.

"Not really." So many tantalizing clues, all leading to dead ends. Sighing, she stuck a fry into her mouth. She wanted to scream, "I suck at this!" but that would be unfair to Emily. What would she do, offer empty words of assurance? Smile sympathetically? Suddenly become interested in her food and wish she were somewhere else? "Maybe I'll email the person," she blurted. "They probably used a throwaway email address, but it's worth a try."

Emily looked at her. "Who do you think the email account belongs to?"

"I don't know. I'm sure the name's fake."

Emily shook her head. "That's not what I meant. Is it someone who can help you find the missing person?"

Hell, yes! "I think they might be responsible for the person going missing."

"You mean you suspect foul play?" Emily's eyes widened. "I thought maybe it was a runaway."

"And the emails were coming from the runaway?"

"Yes. I didn't think you were looking into a criminal matter. Shouldn't the police be handling it?"

Casey chewed on another fry. "They are. Well, they looked into it and didn't get anywhere. They're not even sure a crime was committed. It's still an open case, but I doubt it's getting much attention."

Emily leaned forward to gaze intently at Casey. "Don't email the person."

"Why not?"

"You don't know who you're dealing with. It could be dangerous."

"It's my only lead."

Emily's forehead creased with worry. "Still. Hand over what you have to the police."

Frustration crept into Casey's voice. "I have." How could she explain to Emily that she needed to prove to herself that she hadn't just wasted months of her life, in the face of everyone's skepticism? The long days, the studying, the anticipation of a new start . . . her determination that she wouldn't be Casey in the electronics department forever—at least that had been the theory. If she didn't solve this case, Diane would say *I told you so*, and Ellen would tell anyone who'd listen not to hire the kid who took your money and produced diddly-squat in return. Next time someone phoned about a case—Casey felt like laughing—she'd feel like even more of an imposter than she had when Ellen had called. If she wasn't willing to take risks, to follow every clue until there was nowhere left to go, she didn't belong in this business. "Whatever I send will probably bounce."

"What if it doesn't? And what will it accomplish? As you said, the email address is likely a throwaway. The name on the account is probably bogus."

"I have to do something," Casey snapped, then she winced. "Sorry."

"No, I'm sorry," Emily said softly. "I have no right to meddle."

Casey wanted to say that Emily was only worried about her, but it would sound presumptuous.

"Just be careful," Emily said.

They lapsed into a heavy silence.

"Do you have any pets?" Casey asked, hoping a change of subject would lighten the atmosphere.

Emily chuckled. "I was about to ask if you have any favourite TV shows. I like your question better." She held up two fingers. "Two cats."

"Are they purebreds?" *Please, please, don't let her say they're Sphynxes.*

"No. I got them both from the Humane Society. They're brother and sister. Tiggy and Tippy. Both gray tabbies." She whipped out her phone. A few seconds later, she held the phone out to Casey. "Tiggy's on the left," she said as Casey examined the photo of two tabbies stretched out on the floor, catching the sun. "How about you?"

"We have one cat. Midnight."

"Black?"

Casey nodded. "Yeah, how original. I don't have any pictures on my phone, though," she said, feeling as if she'd let Mid down.

"Did you know black cats are the least adopted from shelters? Same goes for black dogs. Stupid superstitions," Emily muttered. She held out her hand for her phone. "I won't bore you with all the other photos of them." A smile played on her lips. "Not today, anyway."

Casey handed the phone over. So, Emily adored cats. She felt a grin coming on.

"So you and your grandmother have a cat," Emily drawled. She picked up one of her few remaining fries. "I hope you don't mind me asking, but why do you live with your grandmother?" She groaned. "That didn't come out right. What I meant was—"

"Since I'm living with family, why aren't I living with my parents?"

Emily pointed the fry at her. "Right." The fry disappeared into her mouth. She froze. "I hope I haven't just put my foot in it."

"Don't worry, my parents didn't die in an accident when I was three. They're both very much alive." Casey grabbed her napkin and started playing with it. How much should she divulge to the PhD student sitting across from her?

"If it's too personal, I'll understand. I'll ask again when we know each other better," Emily said with a shy smile.

Casey's reticence fled. "After high school, I didn't go on to college or university," she said, still clinging to the napkin. Even now, the compulsion to apologize was strong. "My father and older brother are engineers. My mother is a teacher. My older sister got her bachelors in economics and now she's doing her MBA while working for some hotshot company. I don't remember either one of my siblings getting less than an A or a 90 for anything." Suddenly aware that she was balling the napkin in her hand, she consciously relaxed her fingers. Emily was staring at her, expressionless, probably wondering what any of this had to do with Casey living with Gran.

"I was the C student who didn't know what I wanted to do with my life," Casey continued, hoping she didn't sound bitter. "When I was in my final year of high school, it was one argument after another. They—my parents—kept insisting that I should choose something and try to get into university, that I'd at least have a degree at the end, and hopefully have figured out what I wanted to do. But I didn't want to do that. I didn't see the point." She paused when Emily shifted in her seat, then went on when Emily remained silent.

"They were disappointed." Understatement of the freaking year. "They didn't hold a party when I told them that my part-time job at Walmart would become full time. Around a year after I graduated, they said that if I wasn't going to continue my education, there was no point living at home. I was an adult who was earning. Time to move out. I think they were hoping I'd respond by going to school. I think that's what they were hoping." At least she'd told herself that as she'd digested the reality that her parents were kicking her out. Had their shock run as deep as hers when she'd said that she had no intention of going to university, so she'd start looking for an apartment? Had they intended it to be a bluff?

"I was tired of the constant jabs, anyway." They'd never come out and told her how much she'd disappointed them, but it hadn't taken a private investigator to pick up on all the clues. Two over-achieving children, and one they didn't understand. When they met new people, did they say they had two children, or three? Did they mumble when they explained what their youngest did for a living? Heck, when she'd told them she'd registered for a program to get her PI licence, they'd barely resisted rolling their eyes. She'd thought they'd be proud . . .

"Anyway, I wasn't making much more than minimum wage, and I realized that I'd either have to find a roommate, which I didn't want to do, or live in a dump. That's when Gran stepped in. I was moaning about my apartment search and she suggested moving in with her. She said I was over there half the time anyway," Casey said with a self-deprecating chuckle.

"Escaping from the home front?" Emily said.

"Not entirely. I'd usually drop in on her after work to see if she needed anything, and I'd end up staying for dinner and watching some TV with her." Casey shrugged. "When she suggested it, I wasn't crazy about the idea. Who wants to live with their grandmother? But the more I thought about it, the more I figured it would help both of us, and she kept bringing it up. So I moved in."

"That was . . ."

"Three years ago." And despite Gran's bluster, she'd never once hinted that Casey should go back to school, or shown any disappointment in her youngest grandchild. Casey had arrived on Gran's doorstep with all of her possessions except her bike stuffed into a carry-on luggage bag and two knapsacks. Gran had seen through her fake grin and enveloped her in a bear hug. "Thank god it's you and not your brother or sister," she'd bellowed into Casey's ear. "I don't know what the hell's wrong with your mother. If I hadn't popped her out myself, I'd wonder if she was adopted. Woman's boring as all hell, marries a man boring as all hell, and has two kids who are boring as all hell. When you came along, I thought, 'Finally, someone like me.' If I didn't know for a fact that your mother gave birth to you, I'd wonder if *you* were adopted." And then she'd patted Casey's back while Casey had a little cry on her shoulder.

"So that's the story." Casey swallowed. "I want to make this PI thing work. Not to win my parents' approval." That was a lost cause. No, she wanted to do it for herself and Gran, who hadn't blinked when Casey had said she'd quit her job when she got her licence. "Don't worry about your share of the rent for a while," Gran had simply said, referring to Casey's meagre contribution. She couldn't let Gran down. She'd give it her all, and if it didn't work out, she'd knock on every store manager's door until someone gave her a job. Whatever her parents thought of her, she wasn't a freeloader. "I want to make it work because it's what I want. It's also why sitting here is the closest I'll ever get to university." Might as well make it clear now that whenever she was asked what level of education she'd attained, she'd check the box next to *High School* for the rest of her life.

"Oh, I don't know, maybe you'll visit my closet—otherwise known as my office." Emily sipped her iced tea. "How did your mother feel about your grandmother taking you in?"

"She said it was typical." Among other things, such as Gran was half the problem, and Gran didn't value higher education. Bullshit. Gran and Granddad had remortgaged their freaking house to put Mom through university. And what had they gained for their trouble? A daughter who looked down her nose at them. Why couldn't Mom understand that not everyone wanted the same things from life? "They talk, but I wouldn't call them close."

"I wonder how your parents would view my father." Emily quirked a brow. "He didn't graduate from high school, but he has a sharp mind for business. Bought his first franchise when he was twenty-five, using a loan from his parents and money he'd scraped together working two jobs and doing whatever anybody wanted doing—mowing lawns, fixing leaky faucets, shovelling snow. You name it, he did it. Now he owns his own chain of coffee shops, and all sorts of people come to him for business advice. I have a lot of respect for him."

Casey silently thanked her. Maybe there was hope for them, after all. "I assume he didn't kick you out because you wanted to go to university."

Emily laughed; her flushed cheeks and bright brown eyes set Casey's heart racing. "No, he didn't. Even if he'd wanted to, my mother wouldn't have let him."

Casey envied her. She would have settled for having one parent on her side. "You moved out to be closer to school."

Emily's face slackened. "Sort of." Her eyes avoided Casey's.

Amazing, how someone could go from appearing carefree to uncomfortable within a second. "Do your parents know you're gay?" Casey asked, wondering if Emily was hiding it from them, or they'd found out and life at home had become difficult.

"Oh yeah, and they're totally okay with it. Moving out had nothing to do with them." Emily folded her arms and leaned forward to rest them on the table. "I'm being completely unfair. You told me your moving out story, and now I'm hesitating to tell you mine." She sighed. "The thing is, your story made it clear that you knew what you wanted, or didn't want, and despite all the pressure, you stuck to your guns. That's admirable. Mine will just make me look stupid."

"I'm sure it's not that bad," Casey said, dying of curiosity.

"Trust me, it's that bad."

She wanted to reach out and squeeze Emily's arm, but settled for squeezing the napkin instead. What could it be? A woman. "Did you move in with someone?"

For some reason, Emily's mouth turned up at the corners, but her eyes remained dull. "No. Do your parents know you're gay? Your grandmother does."

"Yeah, they know," Casey said, aware that Emily was changing the subject. "They were like, okay, but are you going to university?" When Emily chuckled, Casey decided not to pry any further about her reason for moving out. "I'll ask you why you moved out when we know each other better."

Emily's gaze lingered on Casey's face. "You do that."

Her breath caught in her throat at the vulnerability and gratitude in Emily's eyes. She reached for her Coke and gulped some down, her gaze still on Emily.

THE MAN WHO'D taken Jackie from the hospital was a friend, not a foe, Casey concluded as she sat on her bed, stroking Mid. After all, if someone had wanted to harm Jackie, why remove her from the hospital? And if someone wanted to kill her, why do it in a way that drew the police's attention? Well, there wouldn't be a body to autopsy; no body, no homicide case. That was why it was a missing person case.

Jackie had been in a coma, with no signs of coming out of it. Maybe the murderer was afraid of what she'd say if she regained consciousness. Wait, maybe the coma was the result of a murder attempt! Maybe whatever had caused Jackie's cramps was supposed to have killed her. Maybe Steve Rose *was* a foe, and when Jackie had survived and ended up in a coma, he'd moved on to Plan B.

Casey didn't believe it. There was the power of attorney, and the fact that Steve Rose had gone through the trouble of kidnapping a comatose Jackie. Could the cops be right about the power of attorney being genuine? What if Jackie had given it to Steve? What if she'd suspected that something bad might happen to her, and she hadn't wanted to involve Ellen? Maybe Steve had worried that someone might kill Jackie as she lay in the hospital bed.

Who was Steve to Jackie, and where had he taken her? Why didn't Ellen know him?

The email address of the man who'd met Street was Casey's only potential route to Steve. If she was right and he was on Jackie's side, then sending an email wasn't a risky proposition. But it would probably bounce, and then what? She'd call Ellen, go back to Jackie's house, and search every single room from top to bottom. If only she could get into Jackie's office at work. Mike had said he wanted to help . . . Casey shook her head. She'd try the email first.

She gave Mid one final pat, sprang off the bed, and waved to Gran as she left the apartment. Ten minutes later, she sat at a computer at a local Internet café and created a new email address at one of the free email sites, calling herself *ccs8972*. She opened a blank email, typed in the subject *Important information about Jackie Rose*, and wrote a single line as the body of the email: *I know you have Jackie Rose.*

Casey stared at the blinking cursor at the end of the line, then moved the pointer to the Send button. One click . . . and the email would bounce. Not wanting to lose her nerve, she clicked. Shit, there it went. She waited a few seconds, then refreshed the Inbox. Nothing. Her heart thumped. She refreshed the Inbox again. Still empty. The email hadn't bounced—yet. Feeling as if she were being watched, she signed off and left the café. She'd return tomorrow to check for a bounce email—or a reply.

Chapter Ten

HER ANTICIPATION RISING, Casey locked her bike and hurried into the Internet café. The same guy was at the cash and smirked at her. Let him think she was here to chat with some stud or hang out on an online dating site; what did she care?

She could hardly contain herself as she signed into her new email account. One new email! But it was probably a bounce message—no! She stared at the screen in disbelief. "John Smith" had replied earlier that morning. The email said: *Who are you?* That was it. Who are you?

Casey leaned back in her chair and pondered what to say, then typed *Someone who won't stop looking for Jackie Rose until she finds her, and she's closing in.* She pressed the Send button, then surfed the Net while she waited. If she were him, she'd be checking her email every five minutes. Too bad they couldn't chat; it would speed things up. She'd have to settle for hanging around here between replies. If she was right, they'd soon be emailing back and forth in real time, anyway.

She wasn't surprised when the reply arrived twenty minutes later. *We should talk. What's your phone number?* No way. Did he think she was stupid? She replied: *Let's meet instead. Somewhere public.*

Five minutes later: *You're getting yourself mixed up in something you don't understand. Take my advice and walk away.*

And do what? Inform Ellen that she'd exhausted all leads and her mother was gone for good? Tell Diane that her first case was a bust? Watch her parents exchange knowing looks when she told them she hadn't solved her case? Tell Emily she'd do better with the next one, honest? If Emily no longer wanted to see her, Casey wanted it to be because they weren't a good match, not because Emily thought she was a loser.

Whoever was emailing her knew where Jackie was, or at least had information that would lead to her or explain her disappearance. Casey couldn't turn her back on that. Ellen had hired her to find Jackie, and Casey wouldn't give up until she had. She replied: *I'm going to find Jackie. I know you took her. I know you're a friend. I'm closing in.* If she wasn't emailing Steve Rose, or he wasn't on Jackie's side, she'd lose him, but it was a gamble she had to take. Better to find out now that she had lousy deductive skills and instincts, and would suck at this PI thing.

She didn't have to wait long for a reply: *Can you meet me at Redfield Park at four today? I'll wait for you at the entrance to the flower gardens. What do you look like?*

No, on both counts! For all she knew, the flower gardens could be deserted at that time of day. *I'll meet you at four, but not at Redfield Park. Meet me at Dixon Mall, near the sandwich bar in the ground level food court.* That place was always bustling. *What do you look like?*

His reply: *I'll meet you at Dixon Mall, but you go first on the descriptions. Give me something. I don't know if you're a friend.*

It hadn't occurred to her that he might be afraid to meet her. Had he taken Jackie to protect her? Casey didn't feel comfortable describing herself first, but she needed this meeting. *Female. Brown hair. Slim. I'll be wearing jeans and a hoodie.*

When she received his reply, she swore loudly, drawing looks. *See you at four.* Shit! Now he had the advantage—if she went. Casey stared at the screen and went through the motion of pondering what to do, because she knew in the pit of her stomach that she'd be at Dixon Mall at four. Nothing would happen to her in the middle of a crowded food court, but she felt compelled to let someone know, and she didn't want to worry Gran. She left the café and pulled out her phone.

"Hi," Emily said brightly.

Casey smiled. "This isn't a bad time, is it?"

"No, not at all."

"Do you want to get together tomorrow night?" she blurted, surprising herself.

"Sure. Did you have something particular in mind?"

Since she'd given the matter zero thought . . . "No, I just thought it would be nice to see you."

"Well, I'd like to see you, too. Why don't I pick you up around seven and we'll decide where to go from there?"

"Sounds good." Casey hesitated. "I emailed the guy whose emails you checked out. He replied. I'm meeting him later."

The levity left Emily's voice. "Are you sure that's a good idea?"

"I'm meeting him in a busy public place."

"Still."

"He's my only lead to my missing person, and I'm positive he's on her side."

"What if you're wrong?"

"I'm not."

Silence, then, "What time are you meeting him?"

"Four."

"Take someone with you. I'd go, but I'm teaching a class."

"Taking someone will only scare him away."

Another long pause, then, "Nothing I say is going to dissuade you, is it?"

"No."

"I want you to call me after you've met with him. If I don't hear from you by six, I'll call the police."

What? "Emily, that's not necessary. He's not going to do me in. Seriously."

"Maybe I just want to hear from you again today."

God, even though she suspected Emily was bullshitting—or maybe half-bullshitting—how could she protest against that? "I'll text you."

"No, call me. That's the only way I'll know for sure that you're all right."

"Okay, okay, I'll call you."

"Promise."

"I promise."

"If you get my voicemail, leave a message. I turn off my phone when I'm teaching."

"Okay."

"Where are you meeting him? I'm only asking so we'll know where to start if you disappear."

"I won't! I'm meeting him at Dixon Mall. The place will be packed at that time."

"That's true, I suppose," Emily said, still sounding worried. "Be careful, okay? I'm already looking forward to tomorrow night."

"Me too," Casey said, hearing the strain in Emily's voice and appreciating her effort to hide her concern. "I'll talk to you later," she said, infusing her voice with confidence.

"Talk to you later," Emily echoed. They said good-bye and hung up.

Casey slipped her phone into her pocket and unlocked her bike. For someone who wanted to take things slow, Emily sometimes came across as a serious girlfriend. Since Casey was also unsure about what she wanted, Emily's uncertainty didn't annoy her. Hell, zooming full speed ahead with relationships had gotten her nowhere. Of course her crushes had never lived up to her expectations; they'd dumped her, rather than she dumping them, because she'd been too busy convincing herself that their obvious incompatibilities didn't exist. Who wanted to admit after five minutes of dating someone that she'd wasted months of her life being infatuated with them? Gran was right, she'd made lousy choices. Instead of choosing girlfriends based on physical attraction and the fantasy life she'd built for them, she should be more analytical.

She felt in her bones that a relationship with Emily had potential. Emily was easy on the eyes. Casey enjoyed seeing her. Best of all, she felt comfortable with her. So yeah, she was willing to take it slow and see what, if anything, developed. Maybe behaving all grown-up with Emily would turn out to be the wisest thing she'd ever done, or maybe she'd end up crying into her coffee—and looking for a new coffee shop to buy her coffee from.

But first she had to survive her meeting with the mystery man. With a sigh, she mounted her bike and rode home to bite her fingernails.

CASEY STRODE INTO the food court and surreptitiously looked over at the sandwich bar. Several people were in line, and two guys stood near the counter, likely discussing what to order. Not far from the men, a woman in a jean jacket with her hands in her pockets rocked on her heels. She was probably waiting for someone. A light bulb went on. A woman? Casey had expected Steve Rose. She glanced at her watch: *3:58*. The woman might not be her contact.

There was one way to find out. Casey strolled over to the sandwich bar and scanned the menu hanging behind the counter. She made a show of checking her watch, looked the menu over again, glanced around, and peered at her watch a second time. When she looked up, the woman in the jean jacket had moved closer to her. Their eyes met.

The woman stepped toward her. "CC58972?" she whispered.

What? Oh, right. "Yes." She studied the woman, who couldn't weigh more than one hundred pounds and stood maybe five feet tall. Casey's tension drained away. She could take her.

"Let's move away from the counter. Too crowded," the woman said, motioning for Casey to follow her.

"What's your name?" Casey asked, falling into step with her.

"No names," the woman said tersely.

"Where's Jackie Rose?"

"Not here." They left the food court and joined the throng of shoppers marching from one store to the next. The click of heels on tile echoed in Casey's ears. "I don't want . . . anyone . . . we're saying," the woman said.

"What?"

She grasped Casey's arm and leaned into her. "I said, I don't want to risk anyone overhearing our conversation," she shouted, turning heads, which demonstrated her point. "There's a McDonalds just around the corner. Let's go there."

Casey pulled her arm away. "Okay." The McDonalds would be crowded too, but they wouldn't have to yell at each other.

They exited through the revolving doors, and the woman pivoted right, then turned a corner, Casey trailing after her. An alley. A van—her brain instantly sounded the alarm, but too late. "Hey!" she yelled as two men leapt from the back of the van and grabbed her arms; she struggled futilely as they dragged her into the van, kicking at them and trying to yank her arms free, but the men were strong, and held her tightly.

"Sit down," one barked as they both applied downward pressure. She landed on her rear end with a thud. No cushy seats in the back of this van, just a hard metal floor. No windows, either.

The woman climbed into the van and slammed the door shut. Casey squinted as her eyes adjusted to the dimness. "Don't bother," the woman said when she noticed Casey's narrowed eyes. She lifted the hood draped over the back of the passenger seat and approached Casey. "Do what we say and you won't be hurt."

Casey wanted to kick her, but she sat still and tried not to hyperventilate as the woman slipped the hood over her head, plunging her into darkness. "On your knees. Hands behind your back," one of the men growled. She complied, and felt the handcuffs snap into place.

You know, maybe this PI thing wasn't for her. She could be showing someone to the aisle with the latest must-have gadget right now. Not the most exciting way to spend one's time, but she could do without the excitement of kneeling in the back of a van, blind and handcuffed, with a bunch of strangers who'd probably kill her. Shit!

The van moved. Someone slipped Casey's wallet from her pocket. "Casey Cook," the woman murmured a moment later. Then, "And you're a private investigator. Interesting."

Casey seethed when someone manhandled her again and removed her phone and notebook from their hiding places. "Who are you?" she asked, not wanting to come across as a complete pushover.

Nobody answered.

"Where are we going?"

"Maybe we should have gagged her," one of the men said.

"At least she's not screaming or weeping," the woman said. "I hate it when they weep."

Cripes, how many people had she kidnapped?

"The screamers I just whack across the mouth," the woman continued. "That usually shuts them up. Doesn't work with the weepers. The wailing gets worse. Sometimes a whack turns a screamer into a weeper, but it's a risk I have to take."

"Did you have any trouble?" the other man said.

"No. She sized me up and concluded I wasn't a threat. Works every time."

Casey kicked herself. How could she have been so stupid? *Note to self: if I get out of this alive, don't fall for the oldest trick in the book again.*

"At least she's finally shut up."

"Yeah," the woman agreed. "If I couldn't see her heart leaping from her chest, I'd check to make sure the hood isn't suffocating her."

Okay, so she was terrified, but this was the first time she'd been kidnapped. They could cut her some slack. Time to tune them out and worry about her predicament. Where were they taking her? Would she have a chance to plead for her life, or were they driving her out of the city to make her dig her own grave?

She'd been so sure that Steve Rose was a friend, unless . . . maybe the person who'd contacted Street wasn't Steve Rose or associated with him. No, that didn't make sense. Why would someone else make sure Ellen wouldn't be around when Steve took Jackie from the hospital? They had to be in cahoots with each other, and maybe Casey had gotten it all wrong and Steve had removed Jackie from the hospital to kill her. Maybe her instincts sucked and she should give up on her fantasy of being a crack PI before she got hurt—assuming she survived this experience. Given the choice of dying, or having to face everyone and say, "Yes, you were all right, the PI thing was a dumb idea," she'd suck it up and take the second option.

She yelped when the van hit a pothole and launched her a couple of inches into the air, and winced when she landed on her bum with a thud. Those around her chuckled.

"Don't worry, not long now," the woman said.

Casey's spirits lifted. They weren't driving out to a wooded area. But then again, plenty of people were murdered in cities.

Around five minutes later, the van hung a right and stopped. The back door opened, then shut. Someone coughed. The van lurched forward, then rolled to a halt. The engine died. The back door opened again. "Stand up," the woman said as someone grasped one of Casey's arms and hauled her to her feet. Another hand went to her head to keep her from hitting the roof of the van. "Walk forward a couple of steps." Casey did so. "Step off the van." Casey slid her right foot forward until it hit thin air, then stepped down, onto concrete.

It was quiet. She could tell they weren't outside. Garage? When the one holding her arm guided her through a door and onto carpet, her guess was confirmed. "We're going downstairs," the woman murmured. "Take it slow."

The basement didn't sound good, but they weren't pushing her down the stairs and the woman sounded as if she didn't want Casey to hurt herself. A good sign, or grasping at straws? Casey carefully descended the stairs. As soon as her feet left the last step, she was yanked to her left and pushed down into a chair. Her cuffed hands prevented her from sitting up straight.

Silence, then footsteps approached. "I was expecting someone more . . . formidable," a man said.

Someone snorted. "This is Casey Cook, private investigator," the woman said.

The man grunted. "Good work."

"Thanks. Can I go now? I have to pick up Caesar from doggy daycare. He pouts if I'm late."

"What about us?" one of the men who'd captured her asked. "I don't think we need to stick around."

"I agree," the woman said with a chuckle.

Casey stifled a feeble retort as humiliation competed with indignation. Jesus, was she that pathetic? Maybe she could take the new guy.

"Go, go," the man, who was apparently in charge, said. "Wait!" he barked. "The key."

"Oh, right." Shuffling. "Here's her stuff, too."

Casey listened as those leaving clomped up the stairs. She slid one of her feet along the ground and suspected that the floor was concrete. An unfinished basement? A door swung shut. Silence. Panic stabbed through her. Had everyone left? She heard a scuffle. No. The leader—Steve Rose?—was still here. A creak from overhead told her that someone was upstairs, too. Now the sounds of ruffling paper. Was he going through her wallet, or her notebook?

"I'm going to remove the hood, Casey. You can scream as loudly as you like, but it won't do you any good. Nobody will hear you."

Suddenly light assaulted her eyes. She squinted at her surroundings and, despite her predicament, felt pleased with herself. She was in a bright but unfinished basement. A man stood in front of her, the hood dangling from one hand. Forget about leaping to her feet and rushing him. He was at least six feet tall and two hundred pounds, and his biceps strained against his business suit's fabric. She'd hardly make a dent.

Not wanting to appear too interested in him, she shifted her attention to the only piece of furniture she could see: a table, on which her wallet, notebook, and phone sat next to a crowbar. Her stomach sank.

Steve—she'd call him that because he fit Steve Rose's description—dropped the hood next to the crowbar and stared down at her. "Who are you working for, Casey?"

She mustered her courage and stared back at him. After a long moment, he picked up the crowbar and gently slapped it against his other hand as he spoke. "Who are you working for?" he said quietly

Okay, this was getting serious. How far should she go to protect Ellen? A broken leg? Two? This wasn't what she'd had in mind when she'd enrolled for her training. *Dear Universe, if I get out of this in one piece, I promise I'll have a look at a university calendar. I'm not saying I'll go to university, but I'll consider it. I'll seriously consider it, I promise. Thank you.* She flinched when Steve raised the crowbar. He lowered it and touched its end to her cheek. "Next time, it'll come down a lot harder. Who are you working for?"

The floor overhead creaked again, this time louder. Casey had the feeling someone was hovering near the top of the stairs.

"I'm going to count down from five," Steve said. "Five . . . four . . ."

Shit, what should she do? She wasn't James freaking Bond. You know in the movies when the hero has been captured, stabbed, burned, electrocuted, water boarded, and is now chained to a pole and coming in and out of consciousness, but he still manages to figure out a brilliant plan to take down the four guards packing machine guns? When the hero manages to somehow get one of the guards to shoot another one, then strangles the third guard with his feet while simultaneously shooting the remaining two guards in the forehead with a machine gun he's holding with his broken hand? Well, that wasn't her.

"Three . . ."

Respiration rate, increasing. "Okay, okay, I'll tell you."

"Two . . ."

Hyperventilation, imminent. "I'll tell you! Ellen Myers. I work for Ellen Myers."

"Ellen?" someone cried. Then, "I'm coming down."

Casey resisted the urge to glance over her shoulder as the woman descended the stairs. The newcomer strode to Steve's side. Casey's mouth dropped open as she locked eyes with the woman standing in front of her: Jackie Rose.

Chapter Eleven

"Jackie rose!" casey blurted.

"No, I am Petrova Romanovich, Russian spy," Jackie said, with a thick accent.

Casey gaped. "Are you serious?"

Jackie laughed. "No, I'm not. But I've always wanted to say that." She turned to Steve. "What did you think of the accent?"

He hesitated. "It sounded German to me."

Funny, Casey had thought it was French. She shook herself. "Would somebody please tell me what the hell is going on?"

"Take the cuffs off," Jackie said. "She's working for Ellen. She's not a threat."

Steve fished a key from his pocket and removed the cuffs. Casey rubbed her stiff arms and wrists.

"So Ellen hired you?" When Casey nodded, Jackie smiled and shook her head. "Damn that girl. I knew she'd be worried, but I didn't expect her to hire an investigator."

"Maybe we should have told her," Steve said.

Jackie's eyes bulged. "No! Telling her would have been the same as broadcasting it on the news."

"Broadcasting what on the news?" Casey asked.

They looked at each other. "What are we going to do? She can blow everything." Jackie frowned. "What am I saying? The fact that she's here means we're already screwed. Why couldn't Ellen have found someone incompetent?"

"Ms. Cook found us, so she's certainly no slouch," Steve agreed.

Casey sat up straighter. *Did you hear that, Mom and Dad? No slouch.* She'd solved her case—sort of.

Steve scratched his head. "We can't hold her here. Well, I suppose I could have her arrested for interfering with a government investigation."

"What?" Casey stood. "Look, I was hired to find Jackie. I don't know anything about a government investigation. It's not my fault you left a trail."

"You should have stayed upstairs," Steve said to Jackie. "I would have warned her off and let her go."

"You don't think I would have called the cops and told them about this place?" Casey said.

"What address would you have given them, considering I'd have had you driven out of here with a hood over your head?"

"Well . . ." Good point.

"I didn't think," Jackie admitted. "I miss Ellen. I miss my life. I want this to be over. And now it turns out that it could all be for nothing, because she's going to leave and blow everything."

"Maybe not." Steve turned to Casey. "What does she know? That you're here? Where? Even if she figures it out, by the time they come looking, we'll be gone."

"She'll know I'm not in a damn coma."

"But she'll have no proof. Hey, Ellen, I found your mother. She's alive and well, but I can't tell you where she is. Can I have my big fat cheque, please?"

"Hey, that's not fair." Casey folded her arms. "I don't want to scuttle any government investigation, okay? If you give me a good reason to keep my mouth shut, I'll keep my mouth shut. But when you're ready to come out of hiding or whatever it is you're doing, I want Ellen to know I found you." She wanted to tell the world that she'd done it!

Jackie pursed her lips. "If I promise to tell Ellen you found me—in fact, if I promise to double whatever Ellen's paying you, will you keep this whole incident to yourself? I won't be missing forever. I'll eventually resurface." She gave Steve a sidelong glance. "Hopefully sooner, rather than later," she muttered.

Casey considered Jackie's offer. It would mean bold-faced lying to Ellen for an indeterminate period of time. If the case was about a missing ring, it wouldn't be so difficult. But she'd seen the tears in Ellen's eyes . . . At the same time, if this was a government matter . . . "Tell me why you're here, and then I'll decide. Was your coma faked? Why are you hiding?"

"Don't say anything," Steve growled. "We can't trust someone your daughter picked out of a phone book."

Casey's hands went to her hips. "You could be lying! *You* grabbed me off the street and brought me here. You're the one who can't be trusted. How do I know you work for the government?"

He pulled a leather folder from his inside jacket pocket, opened it, and held it up.

Okay, it looked official, but she had no idea what a corporate espionage investigations department ID looked like. It could be forged, but she doubted it, mainly because her instincts told her to trust Jackie. The name on the ID was Steve Crayburn. The first name, the matching description . . . he must be the guy who'd snatched Jackie from the hospital. "If you're government, why did you use a low-life like Street to book the spa?"

"My boss wouldn't approve the spa booking," Steve said. "He thought it was perfectly okay to leave Jackie lying in a coma until we had what we needed. I didn't agree, so I went ahead with my idea, anyway. I didn't want to use my credit card." He glanced at Jackie. "I paid Street with my own money."

Jackie frowned. "And I'll repay you . . . as soon as I have my life back."

"Okay, okay." Casey waved the ID away.

"What do you know?" Steve asked as he slipped the ID back into his pocket. "Let's start with that."

Casey jutted her chin toward the notebook on the table. "It's all in there."

"That would be helpful, if I could read it. Have you considered using a smartphone to take notes?"

What was wrong with her handwriting? "I like using a notebook. Let me get it, so I don't miss anything." When Steve didn't protest, she retrieved her notebook—and her wallet and phone. Phone! Emily would call the cops at six. Casey glanced at her watch. It wasn't even five yet. She'd wait until she was out of here or until 5:50, whichever came first. "Okay," she said, opening her notebook. "It started when Ellen called me . . ."

Apart from the occasional grunt, Steve and Jackie remained silent as they listened to Casey's account of her investigation. The moment Casey closed her notebook, Jackie said, "Maybe she can help us. She can get to Mike."

"And trap him?" Steve said.

Jackie nodded.

"You still haven't told me what's going on," Casey pointed out. "Your turn."

"About six months ago, I started to suspect that someone in the company was spying for our main competitor," Jackie said, without waiting for Steve's permission. "But I had no proof. Noticing that someone's accessing files they shouldn't need to access for their job isn't proof, especially when they have permission to access those files. Noticing that someone who's never worked late before is now working overtime isn't proof. It was a gut feeling. I figured there was nothing I could do but keep my eyes and ears open. Things would have stayed like that if it hadn't progressed to sabotage."

Casey's interest spiked. "Sabotage?"

"I usually have a lot of freedom when it comes to developing formulas and testing them. All of a sudden, Mike was super interested in the nitty-gritty details. Now, if Mike had left and the new boss was more hands-on, I wouldn't have thought anything of it." Jackie shifted her weight. "But Mike had never shown any interest in the details before. In fact, he'd get irritated when you gave him too many. Then, all of a sudden, he didn't only want to know the formulas, but he was making suggestions. Weird suggestions. Nothing that would harm a pet, but substituting ingredients that would not only lower the nutritional value, but adversely affect the smell or taste? No. Something was fishy—no pun intended. I started to take notes. I raised my concern with his boss. I didn't accuse Mike of spying. I said he was interfering with my work."

"What did Donna say?"

Jackie's brows shot up. "That's right, you met Donna."

"And her cat."

Jackie grimaced. "Poor thing needs a fur coat. Anyway, Donna didn't take me seriously. She said I should be pleased—pleased!—that Mike was taking more of an interest in my work. Excuse me, but he was ruining my work. Ruining it!"

Casey and Steve made sympathetic noises.

"To add insult to injury, Donna said I should give Mike a break, that he was under a lot of pressure. God, I wanted to slap her. I hate management."

"Since management didn't seem concerned, she contacted my department," Steve said.

"My first thought was to go to security, and I did," Jackie said. "But they were useless. They kept telling me that it wasn't their job to deal with office politics. I wanted to tell them I suspected Mike was spying, but I didn't want to throw serious accusations around when I had no proof. And you start to get paranoid, you know? I didn't know who to trust, who was working for the enemy. Anyway, Steve was assigned to my case. He agreed that something fishy was going on. I started to record my meetings with Mike—on the sly, of course."

"In the meantime, we were trying to find a tangible connection between Mike and the rival company. Money, meetings, that sort of thing. We couldn't find anything." Steve's lips pressed into a thin line.

"But I was putting pressure on him by pushing back on his suggestions and dragging my feet," Jackie said. "I could see it was stressing him out." Her mouth twisted. "I guess his other employer didn't like the lack of results. So he decided to take matters into his own hands. And I caught him. Unfortunately, he also caught me."

"What do you mean?" Casey asked.

"The idiot actually went into the lab to fiddle with my work! I walked in on him." Jackie pressed her hand against her chest. "We stared at each other. He started to babble. I tried to pretend I thought it was all innocent and he was merely trying to help. I guess I didn't quite pull that off, because a couple of days later, I was summoned to see Jerry—Donna's boss. Guess what? They've noticed suspicious activity on the network, and it's me. Access to the network restricted while they do their investigation. Access to the lab restricted—working hours only. I could see what was coming from a mile away. Mike was setting me up to take the fall for him."

"Wouldn't that mean the spying would stop, though?" Casey asked. "In doing so, he tipped off the company."

"What does Mike care? He's already got whatever they're paying him." Jackie scowled. "Money, maybe stock, who knows? Bastard."

"It might not have stopped the spying," Steve added. "We also suspect that Jerry might be involved. He's not only Donna's boss, he's the owner's brother." His eyes narrowed. "We're not sure who got involved first, Mike or Jerry. Apparently Jerry has always resented his older brother."

"Apparently?" Jackie cried. "You can see Jerry's hate burning in his eyes whenever the two of them are in the same room. He thinks daddy should have left him the company. Idiot."

"He can't have the company, so he wants to ruin it." Casey would never understand the "cut off your nose to spite your face" crowd. "So who tampered with the food at the company party?" she asked.

They both stared at her. "Nobody," they said in unison.

Okay, she was totally confused. "But—"

"Someone did something to my lunch," Jackie said. "It would have been next to impossible to tamper with the reception food and guarantee that only I'd eat it. Whatever he used, he knew it would kick in during the party."

"What did you have for lunch?"

"The party wasn't the only celebration that day. The company catered lunch for our department, because we were celebrating someone's work anniversary. I guess my beef came with an extra seasoning that nobody else got," Jackie said wryly.

"And it put you into a coma?"

"No. The doctor did."

Okay, she was totally confused. "But—"

"The coma was induced," Steve said. "Mike wasn't the only one getting a fat bonus."

"A doctor deliberately put you into a coma?" Casey's voice conveyed her incredulity. "Over cat food?"

"This is a serious business," Jackie snapped. "Pet food is a billion dollar industry. We're talking high stakes, here."

"Why not kill you?" Casey asked.

Jackie snorted. "Someone's missing a pair of balls, that's why."

"We figure they intended to keep Jackie out of action until their plan was too far along for her to throw a wrench into it," Steve explained. "Too many Fluffys would already have turned their noses up at the new, improved formula, and she'd be the scapegoat."

"Yes, not only do they put me into a damn coma, but then they spend their sweet time setting me up. Bastards," Jackie muttered. "Fortunately Steve arranged to move me. It only took him a month."

"These things take time," Steve murmured. "There was the power of attorney to forge, the doctor to investigate . . . unfortunately he slipped through our fingers before we had enough evidence to arrest him," he added, for Casey's benefit. "I guess he took the money and ran. He's probably relaxing on some beach, in a country that doesn't have an extradition treaty with us."

"I was hoping to keep Ellen out of it until it was safe for me to reappear," Jackie said. "I can't believe she hired an investigator."

"She loves you," Casey said. "You didn't think she'd stop looking for you, did you?"

"No, but I thought she'd leave it to the police, not hire a crack PI."

Crack PI? Casey was really warming up to Jackie. "When I spoke to Donna, she said that Mike was going crazy because you're away. His job depends on the success of the next new formula to hit the shelves."

"Trust Donna to misinterpret the situation. Mike's job might depend on the formula being a success, but he's depending on it being a failure. He'll falsify the test results and turn in reports that say the formula is a hit with our test subjects. When the food is released and the shit hits the fan, he'll retire on his big fat hidden bank account. As for me, I'd miraculously come out of my coma in time to take the rap."

"But then you disappeared." Casey pondered the angles. "On the one hand, I guess that would benefit Mike and any accomplices. On the other, they have no idea what's happened to you. You could be dead, you could still be in a coma, you could have escaped to a tropical island, or you could be doing what you're doing now—cooperating with a government investigation."

"And that's exactly why poor Mike is frazzled. I hope not knowing is keeping those bastards up at night," Jackie growled.

"Mike called her, so he's obviously worried," Steve said to her.

"Yes, and that's why she might be able to help."

Steve gazed at Casey. "We still don't have enough evidence to bring Mike in. We can't get anyone inside the company, because Jerry's tightened security. But you can get to Mike. You can tell him you have information about Jackie. Meet with him. We'll wire you. Get him to say something incriminating."

How was she supposed to do that? "Uh, this is a guy who put someone he knows into a coma. What's he going to do if someone he doesn't know pisses him off?"

"Tell him you want to go in with him," Steve suggested. "Tell him you'll give him information about Jackie if you get a piece of the pie. Make him see you as being on his side, rather than as a threat."

"I want to go home." Jackie crossed her arms across her chest. "I want to see my cats—and Ellen. I want to see Sissy, before she makes an ass of herself with Kenny."

Casey bit her tongue. The boat had already sailed on that one.

"I want to go grocery shopping, for god's sake," Jackie continued. "Most of all, I want to stop their plan before the food ends up on the shelves."

"Can't you analyze the food and get them that way?" Casey said to Steve.

"They won't be poisoning the cats. There's no law against cat food that doesn't taste good, any more than there's a law against people food that tastes bad."

If there was, Casey could think of a few cooks who'd be on the most wanted list. Her sister's meatloaf would earn her life behind bars.

"You can sue a restaurant for making you sick. You can't sue it if the food isn't good." Jackie stepped toward Casey. "Do you have a cat?"

"Yeah. Her name's Midnight. She's black."

Jackie's face scrunched up. "Midnight. That's, uh, cute. What do you feed her?"

"She occasionally gets food from your company," Casey said truthfully.

"Then you'll appreciate the gravity of the situation. Imagine how traumatized Midnight would be, and you, if you fed her food that tasted horrible. Just horrible. She might never touch canned food again. So if you won't snare Mike for me, do it for Midnight, and for all the other Midnights out there. Do it for them."

Should she tell them that she'd do it because she wanted to close her case and shout from the rooftops that she, Casey Cook, was a kick-ass private investigator? Nah, let them believe she was noble. Part of her didn't want cats to consume icky food. But a bigger part of her wanted this case over with. "Okay, I'll do it."

"Yes!" Jackie grinned. "I knew you would."

Steve pointed toward the steps. "Let's go upstairs and discuss the plan. My feet are killing me."

"I'll meet you up there," Casey said. "I need to make a quick call first. If I don't, the police will get involved."

Steve raised his brows. "So there *was* a Plan B. Why don't you put in an application with us? We can always use good investigators."

"I'll think about it," Casey said, wondering if she should. A steady job versus having to scrounge up clients . . . yeah, she'd think about it.

"We'll be in the living room."

Casey watched Steve and Jackie climb the stairs, then she pulled out her phone and called Emily. "I'm okay," she said after they'd exchanged greetings. "Met up with the contact, and the information was invaluable."

"So you didn't run into any problems?"

Casey coughed. "Nope."

Emily blew out a sigh. "Well, that's a relief. I imagined you being bundled into a van and driven off to god knows where."

"Really?" Casey snorted. "Why would you imagine that?" The warm, fuzzy realization that Emily had worried about her made her want to pirouette. "I'll tell you all about it tomorrow night. Everything." Forget the coy "it's confidential" line. She suddenly wanted to confide in Emily, to trust her. If they were going to see each other, refusing to discuss her cases in detail would be a drag.

"I'm looking forward to tomorrow night," Emily said huskily.

"Me too." She swallowed. "I'm still with the contact, so I should go."

"Thanks for saving me a call to the cops."

"Anytime." Grinning from ear to ear, Casey hung up and shoved her phone into her pocket.

WISHING SHE DIDN'T have an audience, Casey dialed Mike's number and hoped he wouldn't answer. She'd prefer to leave a message and talk to him later, when Jackie and Steve weren't staring at her.

A click. "Hello."

Damn. "Mike?"

"Yep."

"This is Casey Cook. I'm the investigator looking into Jackie Rose's disappearance."

His voice climbed an octave. "Right. Hi Casey."

"You said to call you if I found anything out."

"You found something?"

"I did better than that. I found *her*." Dead air. She knew he was gaping.

"I'm sorry, did you say you found her?" Mike sputtered. "You found Jackie?"

"I know where she is, yeah." His stunned silence was oddly satisfying. "But I don't want to talk about it on the phone. We should meet."

"Uh, sure. Let's get together tonight."

Oops, too eager, Mike. "I can't make it tonight. The earliest I can meet you is Thursday night," she said, ignoring Steve's frantic hand waving and Jackie's frown. Casey wanted time to review her notes, and she wanted her evening with Emily before meeting Mike. After discussing the operation, as Steve called it, with him and Jackie, she was confident that she wouldn't be in danger, but a couple of days waiting wouldn't hurt; in fact, Mike stewing for a while could lead to him being careless when they met.

"You sure? You don't even have five minutes to spare?"

"I have more to tell you than just Jackie's location. I've discovered quite a lot."

"I see."

She could hear his wheels turning. Good, adding a dash of panic and apprehension to his brewing impatience would rattle him even more. "Why don't we meet at The Cog, that family restaurant near your work?" she said, offering Jackie's suggestion. They needed a quiet location for the wire, which eliminated coffee shops and food courts. "Say, six o'clock?"

"On Thursday? Sure. I'll make a reservation."

"That would be great. See you then."

"Yeah." Silence. He didn't seem to want to hang up.

"Bye." Casey disconnected.

"Why can't you meet him tomorrow?" Jackie asked.

"Let him stew. It'll give Steve more time to prepare."

"He doesn't need—"

"It's only two days, Jackie," Steve said. "This morning you were potentially looking at weeks, even months."

"True," she said, her mouth pinched.

Steve shifted his attention to Casey. "We'll meet a couple of hours beforehand, to go over the plan and get you wired up. What's your cell number?" As Casey recited it, he tapped it into his phone. "I'll call you Thursday morning."

"Can I leave now? Where are we? My bike is back at the mall."

"I'll call you a cab," Steve muttered. While they waited for it, he handed Casey forty dollars. "That should cover the fare."

She pocketed the bills, figuring that forty dollars wouldn't be enough to get from the burbs to downtown. The van must have driven around in circles. Her suspicion was confirmed when the cab driver pulled away from the curb and she asked him, "What street are we on?" She'd already memorized the house number. "My friend drove me here and I wasn't paying attention."

"Fields Avenue," the driver said, eyeing her in the rearview mirror.

Yep, only about ten minutes from the mall, even closer than she'd expected. The forty dollars was generous, but hell, she'd earned it.

Chapter Twelve

CASEY STEPPED TO her right to allow a man walking his two immaculately groomed poodles to pass by on the sidewalk. She hadn't protested when Emily had suggested they go for a walk after dinner, and couldn't remember the last time she'd strolled along the gay village's main strip. Over a steak dinner, she'd told Emily all about the Rose case. She'd glossed over the bumbling into an ambush part, simply saying that the contact had taken her to Jackie's location—not a lie. The hood, the handcuffs, the woman who'd fooled her, the burly men . . . mere details. Emily had listened calmly until she heard about the plan to meet with Mike, at which point her eyes had widened, her mouth had opened, and she'd put down her fork. But then she'd reached for her napkin, dabbed at her lips, and with a determined look, picked up her fork again and stuffed her mouth with mashed potato.

When Casey had ended her story, Emily had praised her. She'd seemed impressed. Part of Casey had puffed out with pride; the other part wondered if Emily's reaction was feigned. After all, they were on a date—Casey thought—and still in the best behaviour phase. Her skeptical side hadn't dampened the glow Emily's words evoked, though, and Casey couldn't believe how relaxed she felt with her. She wasn't mulling over every word that came out of her mouth, wasn't trying to sound like an intellectual, wasn't overly worried about dropping a forkful of food on her shirt. She wouldn't be thrilled if that happened, but she'd laugh it off, rather than feel two feet tall because she'd ruined the date and her life was over.

Could she be herself because she wasn't gaga over Emily, or because they were soul mates? She didn't feel that she'd known Emily all her life or anything like that, but being with Emily was the most natural thing in the world, much more enjoyable than her other early dates, when she was such a bag of nerves that she could hardly remember what had happened—or cringed, if she could.

Her hand bumped into Emily's; without thinking, she grasped Emily's fingers and curled hers around them. When Emily didn't pull her hand away, Casey gave her a sidelong glance. Emily smiled shyly. Warmth surged through Casey; she squeezed Emily's hand and realized that she *was* gaga over Emily, but this was a different type of gaga, grounded by interest based on reality, and not pure lust.

Emily stopped and peered into a store window. "I haven't been in here for a while. I should make a point of dropping by."

Not wanting to let go of Emily's hand, Casey craned her neck to glimpse the store's sign. Used books. "You're into books?"

"Yes, but that's not why I come here. They have a comics section in the back."

"You read comics?"

"I collect them."

"Seriously?" Emily's cool factor shot way up. "Which ones?"

"Anything with Wonder Woman in it. I only started seriously collecting a few years ago," Emily said as they continued walking. "I don't have many old ones. They're expensive. Hundreds, even thousands of dollars."

"Really?"

Emily nodded. "I see the ones I buy now as an investment."

"I bet the bank didn't recommend that," Casey said, recalling the time she'd visited a bank to see if she could put her spare $25.00 a month to work for her. The moment the financial advisor had mentioned starting an RRSP for retirement, she'd tuned out. Retirement? Give her a freaking break. Now, if the woman had brought up comics . . . "I like your style of investing."

"Some people think it's childish."

"Like who?"

Emily took her time answering. "My last . . . I don't know what to call her. Girlfriend, I suppose."

"Oh," Casey said casually.

"She was quite a bit older than me, so maybe she saw a lot of what I did as childish." Emily's hand tightened around Casey's. "She was one of my professors."

A piece clicked into place. "Did you live together, and that's why you moved closer to the university?"

"No to the first part, yes to the second."

Sensing that Emily would say more, Casey waited.

"I was stupid, and naïve, and gullible, and head over heels." Emily let out an exasperated sigh. "I'm being an ass. I'm sure you want to hear all about my last relationship." She tried to pull her fingers from Casey's, but Casey wouldn't let her escape.

"If you want to talk about it, talk about it," Casey said, relaxing her fingers because Emily had stopped trying to get away. "It sounds like you got hurt. What happened?"

"To make a long story short, I had her for one of my classes. Within a few weeks, she was inviting me to her office to discuss my work. That eventually led to discussing it over a coffee, then a drink . . . I'm sure you can guess the rest. I thought she was genuinely interested in me."

"But she wasn't?"

"Maybe she was in the beginning, but she was never interested in having a full-fledged relationship. She saw me as a fling." The quaver in Emily's soft voice made Casey want to hug her. "I should have seen it. I *did* see it. She never stayed over, she dictated when we met . . . I rationalized it away, ignored my friends' warnings, thought I knew best. Can you believe I moved for her?" Emily snorted. "I told myself it would be more convenient for me. Stupid. Anyway, toward the end of the spring semester, she stopped taking my calls. When I dropped by her office, she was always busy. I finally cornered her after a class, and she told me it was over. No emotion, no sorrow, nothing. She'd already moved on."

"You didn't see it coming."

"Nope. Well, deep down I knew."

"And this happened . . ."

"A couple of years ago. When all was said and done, we were together," her voice dropped, "if you can call it that, a little over six months."

And the experience still smarted two years later. A knot formed in Casey's stomach. She waited until they'd crossed a street, then voiced the question on her mind. "Are you still in love with her?"

"God, no! I'm mad at myself. I hate that I let myself be used like that."

"We all lose our minds when we're head over heels. Give yourself a break."

"You might want to save your sympathy. You haven't heard the worst part yet."

Casey turned to her. "What?"

"I found out that she's in a long-term relationship and takes a new pet on the side every year."

"How did you find out?" Casey asked as she digested the information.

"From a former pet, believe it or not. We should form a club. We could probably fill a room."

"She told you to rub it in."

"No. She told me because she saw how miserable I was. I think she was trying to tell me I wasn't the only one. At first I wondered why the hell she'd waited until after it was over to tell me, but now I understand. I wouldn't call up Sandra's current pet and say, 'Hey, did you know she's with someone.' It's not my business, and everyone shoots the messenger," Emily said, frowning.

"You didn't know about her partner, though."

"Of course I didn't know! I wouldn't want someone having an affair with my partner, so I certainly wouldn't do it to anyone else. When I found out, I felt terrible—and stupid. I'd dreamed about us growing old together, and all along, she was going home to someone else." Her anguished eyes met Casey's. "How could she do that? How could she lead someone on like that, knowing it's all a lie?"

"I don't know."

"I'm glad you don't know."

"Not everyone is like that."

"I know." Emily grimaced. "Now I'm a little gun shy about relationships. I always wonder now—not that there's been anyone since then. Not beyond a single date, anyway." She looked down at their intertwined fingers. "I hope I haven't blown things by telling you that I was the other woman."

If Casey didn't want to see anyone who'd made a mistake, her list of potential girlfriends would be empty. In this case . . . "You didn't know you were the other woman. As far as worrying that this relationship will go the same way . . ." Yeah, this relationship, damn it. "I wouldn't. Even if I was like her, if this relationship goes the same way for me as it usually does, you'll dump me in around two or three dates anyway, so I wouldn't worry." She flushed when Emily laughed. Cripes, had she actually said that? Normally she wouldn't be so candid. She'd be doing her best to come across as suave and sophisticated—and failing badly. "I've made some bad choices myself. This time feels different."

"It does," Emily said softly.

Casey resisted the urge to pull Emily closer and kiss her. She'd let Emily set the pace, rather than rush it. Unlike her other relationships, the urgency to move everything to the next level wasn't there, not because she didn't desire it, but because she somehow knew it would happen at exactly the right moment. Yep, something was different about this one, which both excited and scared the crap out of her.

"About this meeting with that woman's boss . . ." Emily said, bringing Casey back to their conversation. "Be careful."

"I won't be alone. Steve will be listening."

"Still. That guy put a woman into a coma. If he figures out you're trying to bust him, what will he do to you? Are you sure you should do it?"

"I want to do it. It'll close my case. That's important to me."

Emily's brow furrowed. "What about that detective you told me about? Maybe you should tell her."

Walker would only push Casey aside and steal all the glory. Casey reluctantly let go of Emily's hand and pulled out her phone and notebook. "I'm adding her to my contacts," she said, making a great show of doing so as Emily watched. "Now she's literally two button presses away, okay? If I sense trouble, I'll call her. I promise." She watched Emily's internal battle flit across her face.

"You're meeting in a public place, right?" Emily said.

"Yeah, The Cog."

"It'll still be light outside."

"We're meeting at six, so yeah," Casey said, struggling to keep her frustration out of her voice. Hey, Emily cared about what happened to her. That was good.

"All right. I guess you've got it all covered. You'll have to tell me all about it afterward."

"I will." Casey said, marvelling at how great it felt to know that Emily was interested in her work. Her heart pounded when Emily slipped her arm through hers and leaned into her as they continued to stroll. Emily had no need to worry about Casey's meeting with Mike, because Casey had no intention of getting hurt. She had a girlfriend, you know. Nothing would stand between her and seeing Emily again.

CASEY TRIED NOT to fidget as the technician prepared her for the meeting with Mike. "We're done," the technician said, stepping back. She waited as Casey carefully slipped back into her blouse and threw on her hoodie, then motioned for Casey to follow her from the bedroom.

"Ready?" Steve said when they entered the living room in the house on Fields Avenue.

The technician jutted her chin toward a man wearing a headset and holding a receiver. "Say something," he growled.

Casey cleared her throat. "Uh, hello. Testing."

He flashed a thumbs-up. Jackie leapt up from her spot on the sofa. "Oh my god, I can't believe I might go home tonight."

Yeah, no pressure or anything. Casey didn't know who she'd piss off more if she screwed up: Jackie, or Steve.

"Remember, we only need him to incriminate himself for tampering with the food, or bribing the doctor, or spying for the competition. We don't need all three," Steve said.

Right. "What should I do if he makes me?" Casey asked.

"If he catches on, or you're worried about your safety in any way, say, 'It's hot in here.'"

"It's hot in here? Isn't that kind of lame? What if it's not hot? What if the air conditioning is going full blast and everyone's shivering? What if it *is* hot and I accidentally say it's hot?" Since she knew she shouldn't say the phrase, it would keep popping into her mind.

Steve frowned. "It has to be something innocuous that you can drop into the conversation at any time. Even if it's freezing, you can say it. Mike will think you're weird, that's all."

"If I say it, you'll come into the restaurant, right?"

"A couple of agents will already be inside, and we'll be right around the corner, under a minute away." He turned to the technician in the headset. "It's time to get this show on the road."

Chapter Thirteen

THE VAN CARRYING Casey and the agents pulled over on a street a couple of blocks away from the restaurant. Casey rolled her bike from the back of the van and turned to Steve. "Is this thing still working?"

"Stop looking down at it," Steve snapped.

"Sorry."

"Don can hear you," he said, looking past her, then he glanced at his watch. "You'd better get going. Good luck."

She smiled weakly and mounted her bike. Unfortunately, in all the fuss she'd forgotten her helmet at the house, but the restaurant was only a short ride away. She'd insisted on using her wheels, so she could quickly escape if she spotted anything suspicious when she arrived. Yep, the more backup plans, the better. Case in point: as soon as she turned the corner, she braked and slipped her phone from her pocket, brought up her contacts, selected Walker's number, and slid the phone into her hoodie's pocket, ready to use. Now Detective Walker was only a button press away. All Casey would have to do was slide her hand into her pocket, feel around, and hope she didn't inadvertently change the contact to someone else, like Gran. Despite her nerves, she smiled, imagining Gran bellowing into the phone at home—which would probably be bad for Casey, since the entire restaurant would hear her, including Mike.

Her stomach churned. *Relax.* They'd worked out what she'd say to Mike that might provoke him into incriminating himself. Over a nice dinner, she'd bore him by telling him all sorts of irrelevant information she'd uncovered, then go for the jugular when his eyelids were sagging. What could go wrong?

Mike not showing up, for one thing. After locking her bike, she strode into the restaurant, expecting him to be waiting for her. But he wasn't there, and a scan of the main dining room came up empty. Nobody matched Mike's photo. There were supposedly two agents here, but Casey couldn't pick them out. Was it the man and woman chatting over a pizza? The two men ignoring each other as they texted on their phones?

A woman hugging a stack of menus to her chest beamed at Casey. "Can I help you?"

"I'm meeting someone, but I don't see him. He might be in the other dining room."

The woman shook her head. "We haven't opened it yet. Do you have a reservation?"

"Yeah. Mike Hargrave."

She checked the book. "He hasn't arrived yet. Have a seat." She swept her free arm toward a cushioned bench and winked. "Don't worry. He'll be here."

He'd better be. Should she try to murmur surreptitiously that Mike hadn't arrived? No, they'd gather that from her conversation with the greeter. Forget the wire, already. Damn, she hated waiting. More time to think about what could go wrong. *It's hot in here.* No! Well, yeah, it was a little warm, but no!

She twisted to look out the window. Shit, there he was, strolling toward the entrance. Casey stood, then sat, not wanting to appear eager. She watched as he approached the *Wait Here to Be Seated* sign, then counted to five, rose, and said, "Mike Hargrave?"

He spun around.

"Casey Cook." Hoping to exude confidence, she stepped toward him and held out her hand.

"Pleased to meet you, Casey."

The greeter reappeared. "This way." She led them to a table in the middle of the dining room and set two menus down.

"Can we have one near a window?" Mike asked.

"Sure," she chirped, picking up the menus. "This way."

"Thank you," Mike said as he slid into the window booth.

"No problem." As the greeter turned to walk away, she raised her brows at Casey.

Oh, please. Mike was old enough to be her father.

"So you said you know where Jackie is," Mike said.

Wow, he wasn't wasting any time. "I know how to get to her."

Mike's brow furrowed. Good, she'd meant it to be cryptic. "To explain what I mean, I'll have to tell you how I found her. Let's wait until we have our food, so we won't be interrupted."

He didn't protest. They studied their menus. When the waitress came over to see what they wanted to drink, they told her they were ready to order. Then they made awkward small talk until the waitress had placed their pasta dinners in front of them, made sure they had everything they needed, and left.

Mike lifted his fork. "So how'd you find Jackie?"

In painstaking detail, Casey told him how she'd located Jackie, a mixture of truth and fabrication. She could tell that Mike was busting for her to get to the point, but he didn't hurry her along. He didn't ask any questions, either. He was interested in only one thing, and as she swallowed her last noodle and placed her knife and fork on her empty plate, she finally got to it.

"So I met my contact, and he had an interesting story to tell. About you." She let that sink in, though Mike remained expressionless. "He said you *put* Jackie into a coma." No reaction. This wasn't going as Casey expected. "He showed me a photo of Jackie. He definitely has her. He said either you cut him in on the action, or he'll kill her and make sure the trail leads to you." Mike didn't even twitch. Jesus, was he unflappable? "I figured, why not me, too? I'm sure your offer will be more generous than Ellen Myers' payments."

Mike straightened. "You're blackmailing me?"

"I see it more as joining your team and staying silent out of loyalty."

He stared at her.

"If you're not interested, no problem. I'll turn my information over to the police."

Mike tugged at his shirt collar. "It's hot in here."

It's hot in here? *It's hot in here?* She hoped her panic didn't show on her face. There was no way he could be wired, was there? No, no, what were the chances he was wired *and* had the same SOS phrase? God, she'd known it was too generic, and now desperately hoped that Steve's agents wouldn't come leaping over tables and interrupt just as Mike was starting to sweat. They knew *she* had to say it, right? "I'm not hot," she said loudly and clearly.

"I am."

Casey sensed someone behind her. She twisted to look. Great. The two men she'd seen texting were standing at her elbow. Stupid. *You were supposed to wait for me to say it!*

One gazed down at her. "On your feet, Cook. You're coming with us."

The other one looked over her head. "Pay the bill and meet us outside," he said to Mike.

What?

"Come on, on your feet," the beefier one said.

Confused, Casey stood. Was this Steve's way of extricating her from the situation?

"Walk casually, Cook, or I'll break your legs."

"Sure, sure," she said, her mind racing. Mike was no longer within earshot. They had no reason to put on an act. These weren't Steve's men, they were Mike's! "You know, Mike was just saying how hot it is in here," she said, walking as slowly as she could. "I agree. It's hot in here. Really hot. Hot, hot, hot. I'm burning up here. I feel like flames are shooting from the top of my head."

"Shut up and keep walking."

Shit! She frantically searched for someone, anyone, who was rising from a table and heading in her direction, but everyone was eating and chatting. Where the hell were they? Wait. Was Steve actually working for Mike, this was some type of double-cross deal, and the agents were Mike's all along? Probably not, but screw Steve. She had stuff to look forward to! It was time for Plan B. As they approached the exit, she reached into her hoodie pocket and hoped she was pressing the right button. What if she got Walker's voicemail? What if Walker couldn't hear what was going on? Casey would have to assume that she'd answered and was listening.

"Dragging me from The Cog and kidnapping me isn't a good idea," she said as she stood outside the restaurant, flanked by the two men.

She could make a run for it, and maybe make it around five feet before they were on top of her and her face hit the pavement. "I told the police I'd be here. They know I found Jackie Rose and you're in on it. As I said, not a good idea to take me from . . . *The Cog* . . . in broad daylight."

"Shut up," Beefy growled. A van pulled up. Great, another van. She was starting to hate vans, though she'd really love to see Steve's van right now. *Around the corner, my ass.* Was something wrong with her wire? Beefy yanked open the van's rear door. "Get in," he growled.

"I've always wanted a . . . *white Ford van*," Casey said as they hustled her inside. Unfortunately, she wasn't in a position to glimpse the licence plate number.

Mike joined them and pulled the door shut. "Tie her hands—and her feet."

"You're crazy . . . *Mike*," she said as beefy complied. "You really think you'll get away with this?"

"The only thing I want to hear out of your mouth is where Jackie is."

"I don't have her exact location. I'll have to call my contact."

His face reddened and he lunged toward her. "Bullshit! You tell me where Jackie is right now, or I'll make you disappear, too."

"Okay, okay," she said, realizing that making them think about phones wasn't a good idea. Forget about giving them the Fields Avenue address. She'd protect Jackie and do what she could to save herself. "She's on a farm in the Valley Ridge area."

"What highway?"

"Uh . . . twelve."

"Go," Mike barked to the driver. He turned his cold eyes back to Casey. "If you're lying, you'll regret it."

She was hoping that someone would come to her rescue during the hour drive. *Please, please, let Walker be overhearing everything.*

The van pulled away and accelerated through the parking lot, tires squealing. Then it screeched to a halt, flinging Casey and everyone else toward the front of the van. If this was a movie, she'd make her move, but in the movies they didn't fall on their asses and roll around helplessly. Plus, they'd already have secretly untied their hands and feet by now, and probably weren't wincing in pain because a phone had dug into their ribs.

"What the hell's going on?" Mike said when the van remained stationary.

"Some crazy chick just drove right in front of me and stopped." The driver leaned on the horn and rolled down the window. "Hey, you! Get out of the way, you stupid moron. What do you think you're doing? Move! Now! Oh, shit."

Mike's face tightened. "What?"

A siren—it sounded like several, actually—answered the question for everyone. Casey's captors glanced wildly at each other.

"Drive!" Mike shouted.

"I can't. That stupid car's blocking my way."

Mike blanched. "Run!"

Beefy almost trampled Casey when he charged from the van. Mike and the other man leapt out. The driver's door slammed shut. Still lying on her side, Casey lifted her head, then sat up. "Hello?" She tried to stand, but her bound feet hindered her. "I'm tied up, here. Anyone? Steve? You there?"

Shouts, then a bang, too loud to be a gunshot. "He ran that way," someone yelled.

"Hello? I'm in here! Tied up!" She tried inching toward the partially open rear doors, but her progress was slow. One of the doors suddenly swung fully open. Good, the cops were finally checking the van. Casey gaped when Emily clambered aboard.

Emily's eyes widened. "Oh my god, are you all right?"

"You're the crazy chick?" Casey sputtered, wondering if she'd hit her head on the way down and was hallucinating.

"Let me untie you."

Casey bit her tongue as Emily freed her, then jumped to her feet, anger conquering her surprise and gratitude. "What are you doing here?"

"I decided to back you up."

"I didn't need backup. I had everything under control."

Emily quirked a brow at the rope lying at her feet.

"I called the cops. I was fine. I didn't need rescuing, thank you very much."

"I didn't interfere until I saw you leaving the restaurant with men who looked shifty." Emily folded her arms. "When they forced you into the van, I did what I thought was best."

"You shouldn't even be here!" Casey slapped her thighs. "What's everyone going to think?"

"That you found your missing person and courageously offered to help another investigation. You closed your case."

"Yeah, and that my girlfriend thinks I can't take care of myself."

Emily's mouth turned up at the corners. "Your girlfriend, eh?"

"Emily!" Casey wanted to . . . hug her.

"Look, I was worried about you, okay? All I intended to do was sit in my car and go home when I saw you leave. That's all."

But then she'd witnessed a kidnapping in progress and thwarted it. How the hell could Casey be mad at her? Thanks to Emily, only her pride was wounded. It could have been worse. Hadn't she hoped someone would rescue her?

"I thought you said agents would be listening in."

"I don't know what happened to them. They were supposed—"

"Don't move!"

They both turned toward the voice. Casey shrank back at the sight of the cop pointing a gun at them. "Hey, I'm the victim here."

"I'm the driver of the car that stopped the van," Emily said, slowly raising her hands.

He squinted at them. "We'll sort it all out down at the station."

"What?" they said in unison.

"Come on, ladies. I won't ask again."

After glancing at Emily, Casey hopped off the van and surveyed the chaos. She counted four cop cars, their lights still flashing. Mike, beefy, and her third captor were in cuffs. "I don't see the driver of the van," she said to the cop, who'd holstered his gun, apparently deciding they weren't a threat.

"He's over there." The cop jutted his chin toward a man sitting on the ground, rubbing his knee. Two cops stood over him. "Lucky guy. He would have been more than nicked if our car hadn't swerved in time. Luckily for him, the car hit the bike rack instead."

"What?" Casey now spotted a fifth police car—and the totalled rack.

"Fortunately, there was only one bike in it."

"Yeah, my bike!"

The cop clucked his tongue sympathetically. "It *was* your bike."

Casey groaned.

"Come on, I'll put you in a car until the detective gets here."

"I've always wanted to sit in a police car," Emily murmured. As soon as the cop slammed the door shut and walked away, she turned to Casey. "Sorry about your bike. But I'm not sorry I came. If I hadn't, who knows what would have happened?"

"You could have been hurt, too," Casey said, not quite ready to forgive all. "What if the van hadn't stopped? What if he'd smashed right into you?"

Emily's mouth pressed into a stubborn line. "All I cared about was stopping them. I wasn't going to let them take you."

Casey tenderly stroked her cheek. "You make it impossible to stay mad at you, you know that?"

Emily swallowed. "You know, kissing for the first time in the back of a police car would make for a good story."

"Yeah, it would." Casey puckered up and—they jumped apart when someone pulled the door open.

Detective Walker peered inside. "Yeah, I can vouch for this one," she said, pointing at Casey. "The other one is the girlfriend."

Casey stared at her. How did she—"

"Christ, the woman saves your ass, and all you can do is whinge," Walker said with a shake of her head. "Will you please hang up your damn phone, already. I've rolled my eyes so much during the last five minutes that I'm afraid I might have permanent eye damage."

Embarrassment proved to be as effective as a cold shower. "I can't believe how fast you all got here," Casey said lamely as she pulled out her phone and disconnected.

"Someone up there must like you. There's a coffee and donut shop right around the corner." Walker jerked her thumb over her shoulder. "Come on out and we'll have a chat."

Casey and Emily obediently slid from the back seat and stood meekly next to Walker.

"You can have a talk with Officer Stanley," Walker said to Emily as she beckoned to a nearby cop. "I'll chat with you, Cook. We might be a while, so maybe you two can meet up later and continue your riveting conversation."

"Sure." Casey turned to Emily.

"I'll call you." Emily flashed Casey a smile and walked away with Stanley.

"All right." Walker leaned against the cop car and fixed steely eyes on Casey. "Start from the beginning, and don't leave anything out."

Twenty minutes later, Casey finished her story. "And then you guys arrived." She shoved her hands into her pants pockets. "I found Jackie Rose."

"Yes, you did." Walker attached her pen to her notebook. "Don't worry, I said I wouldn't steal your thunder." A cop walked up to Walker and murmured to her. Casey leaned forward but couldn't hear anything. "Mikey boy is quite the talker," Walker said when the cop left. "Trying to save his ass, I guess." She slipped the notebook into the bag slung over her shoulder. "Not bad, Cook. But next time, call me, okay? As you can see, we actually show up when you're in trouble. I could have done without the bad soap opera, though."

"Sorry," Casey mumbled. "Can I go now?"

Walker nodded. "You might have to testify in court." She looked past Casey. "Someone wants to talk to you."

Casey turned around. "Steve! Where the hell were you?"

"So this is the crack agent." Walker eyed him up and down, snorted, and said, "You and I need to talk."

"Can it wait until tomorrow?"

"I suppose so." Walker smirked. "There's no rush. We have a confession. Didn't have any trouble at all getting him to talk." She strolled away.

Steve's jaw tightened.

"Where were you?" Casey said again. "Those guys weren't playing around."

Steve waited until Walker was out of earshot. "When you said you weren't hot, the agents inside thought you'd sized up the situation and were instructing them not to move in under any circumstances."

"I said I was being kidnapped. How much of a freaking hint did they need?"

"At that point, they did react, but you were already outside. They decided they'd follow the van, rather than risk you getting hurt."

"Okay, but what about you?"

"Oh." Steve smiled sheepishly. "We were getting a parking ticket."

"What?"

"Those signs are confusing. One pointed to the left and said no parking. The second one said no parking between 10:00 a.m. and 4:00 p.m. The third said parking permitted between 8:00 p.m. and 6:00 a.m. The fourth said—"

Casey grimaced. "Didn't you flash your ID?"

"Have you ever dealt with a parking enforcement officer? They're worse than the cops. He boxed us in."

Oh my god, she'd entrusted her life to idiots.

"The two agents inside had your back. You were okay," Steve said.

Easy for him to say, now that the cops—and Emily—had done his job for him. Oh no! "Um, about what you heard on the wire after Mike and company ran away . . . you can erase that, right?"

"There's nothing to erase. We heard screeching tires and then the transmission went dead."

The wire must have been damaged, or the connection broken, when she was flying around the van. "Can I call Ellen now and tell her that her mother's okay?"

"I think Jackie wants to do that."

She'd better tell Ellen that Casey had found her.

"Let's go back to the house."

"I need to get my bike. I'm hoping it's not badly damaged."

Steve bit his lip. "Oh dear, I forgot about your bike. If it's the one that was in the bike rack . . ." He sombrely shook his head.

Casey walked over to evaluate the damage herself. She stared down at her bike. The poor thing was folded in half and had pretzels for wheels. Buying another one would put her out hundreds of dollars. Shit.

Steve patted her shoulder. "Come on. Let's go tell Jackie she has her life back."

"Okay." Casey silently thanked the mangled hunk of metal for serving her well and trailed after Steve. Her bike was toast, but she'd solved her case, and Emily had almost smashed up her car to save her. Overall, Casey figured she'd come out way ahead—and smiled.

Chapter Fourteen

Back at the Fields Avenue house, Casey squinted out the living room window, but couldn't see far in the darkness. She let the curtain drop and turned away.

"I have goose bumps," Jackie said from the sofa. "I can't wait to see her."

"She shouldn't be long now." Rachel, the woman who'd lured Casey into the ambush outside the mall, crunched on a potato chip. "I'm sure she's dying to see you, too."

Steve grabbed a handful of chips from the bowl on the coffee table. "Have you thought about my proposal?" he asked Casey.

"You mean coming to work for you?"

He nodded and popped a chip into his mouth.

"I think I'll stay independent for now. Maybe when I have more experience under my belt . . ." Meaning that if she was having trouble finding clients, she'd consider knocking on Steve's door.

"You have my card. If you change your mind, call me."

"I will," she said, hoping she wouldn't have to.

Jackie twisted and stared in the direction of the window. "Where is she? Come on, Ellen."

Casey grabbed some chips and squeezed herself onto the sofa. When the doorbell rang, the chip bowl was almost empty.

"I'll get it," Steve said. Jackie stood and covered her mouth with her hands.

Ellen barrelled into the living room. "Mom," she wailed. "Oh my god, Mom."

"Ellen," Jackie cried. They clung to each other and sobbed while the others scooped the remaining chip crumbs from the bowl and watched.

"I'm still so confused," Ellen said, when mother and daughter finally parted. "You're fine. I mean, that's great, but how . . . I mean, you explained some of it on the phone, but I was in shock. I couldn't take it in."

"I'll explain it all to you when we get home," Jackie said, throwing her arm around Ellen's shoulders and squeezing her.

"You look so well."

"I was only in a light coma, so when Steve rescued me, it didn't take long for me to get back on my feet."

"A light coma, eh?" Ellen's face froze. "Could you hear anything while you were in the coma? If you could, anything I might have said about my childhood . . . I was just trying to get a rise out of you, to see if you'd respond to, uh, stuff."

Jackie rolled her eyes. "I couldn't hear anything, so don't worry."

"It wouldn't have mattered if you could, because I didn't say anything bad," Ellen said, her shoulders sagging. Her eyes narrowed at those on the sofa. "Trudy! What are you doing here? Do you two know each other?" she said to Jackie.

Another mystery solved. Casey hoped Rachel had enjoyed her time with Ellen at the spa.

"Ellen, Ellen, Ellen," Jackie said, squeezing her again. "You never cease to amaze me, you know that?"

"Aw, thanks, Mom," Ellen said. "Now, do you know each other?"

Jackie sighed. "I'll explain later. Right now, I think we have an investigator to pay."

"Oh my god, yes." Ellen rushed over to Casey and enveloped her in a bear hug. "I knew you'd find Mom. I'm so grateful."

"No problem," Casey, still sitting, said into Ellen's bosom. Fortunately Ellen let her go before she became light-headed.

"How much do I owe you?" Ellen pulled a chequebook from her purse.

"No, let me," Jackie said. "You've done enough already. I can't believe you hired an investigator."

"Why? You were gone. I did everything I could to find you. I didn't care how much it was going to cost, or how long it was going to take. I was never going to stop looking. Never, ever, ever."

Jackie's lips trembled. "That's my girl." She wiped the corner of her eye and focused on Casey. "I'll just get my chequebook."

"Uh, I have to work out how much you owe me. It'll only take a minute." Casey slid her notebook from her pocket. "If I had to guess, I'd say around a few hundred bucks, but let me add it up."

"Put that thing away. You found me and gave me my life back. Be back in a sec."

"I'm so glad I ran into Alison and Diane that day," Ellen said to Casey while they waited. "And thank you so much for rescuing Mom," she said to Steve. "I didn't take in a lot of what she said on the phone, but I did get that you're Steve Rose."

Steve smiled. "Just doing my job."

Ellen gazed at Rachel. Her hands went to her hips. "Why didn't you call me? Wait. You were working with him, right?" She groaned, then brightened. "But that doesn't mean we can't be friends. We had fun that weekend."

"You can't associate with each other, not until this has been through the courts, anyway," Steve said.

"He's right," Rachel quickly agreed. Casey couldn't tell from her tone whether she was grateful for the excuse Steve had provided.

Jackie bustled back into the living room. "It's Casey Cook, right?" she said, opening her chequebook on an end table.

"Right. I have a question for you."

"What is it?" Jackie asked as she wrote the cheque.

"What was in the envelope taped behind the night stand in your bedroom?"

Jackie lifted her head. "You figured that out? You really are good. Coupons. I have to hide them." She pointed her pen at Ellen. "This one here is always stealing them."

Ellen's face flushed. "No, I'm not."

"Yes, you are. You're too lazy to find coupons yourself. You don't think I didn't notice that every time you visit, some of my coupons go missing?"

"Okay, maybe I took a few now and then. But I haven't taken any for months. I thought you'd stopped collecting them."

"No. I finally found a good hiding place for them."

"I only ever took the extras," Ellen wailed. "Ones you could spare."

"How could you know which ones I could spare?" Jackie shook her head. "Never mind. We've only been back together five minutes and we're already bickering. How quickly the glow fades." She frowned at Casey. "Are you saying my coupons are gone?"

"Yeah," Casey said.

Jackie whirled toward Ellen.

"Don't look at me." Ellen's eyes widened. "It must have been Marge. She's been feeding the cats."

Jackie's lips thinned. "I'm going to have to start storing them in a flipping safety deposit box." She lowered her head again, then ripped the cheque from the chequebook and handed it to Casey.

Holy shit! Was that really four zeros after the number one, or was she hallucinating? "Uh, this is way too much. There's an extra zero and then some."

Jackie snorted. "To me, it's a bargain. You deserve every penny, especially since you met with my sister. Plus, Steve told me about your bike. That should cover a new one."

No kidding. "Th-thank you." Casey carefully folded the cheque and tucked it into her pocket.

"Now, I think it's time for me and my daughter to go home."

"I already left my manager a message saying that I won't be in tomorrow," Ellen said. "We can spend the entire day together."

Jackie's face was a picture of happiness. "That's great. It's, uh, wonderful." She turned to Casey, Steve, and Rachel. "Thank you. For everything. Ellen, let's give Casey a ride home."

"Don't worry about me," Casey said. "You two haven't seen each other for a while. But thanks for offering."

"I'll be in touch," Steve said to Jackie. "Tomorrow is for you and your daughter. I'll call you the day after next."

"You can call me tomorrow, if you like," Jackie said as Ellen tugged at her arm. "Really, you can." She stumbled after Ellen.

"I'm going to recommend you to everyone who needs an investigator," Ellen shouted to Casey before she disappeared into the hallway. "You rock!"

Right now, with her case solved and a cheque for ten thousand dollars in her pocket, Casey didn't disagree with her.

"I can give you a lift home," Rachel said.

Casey still hadn't completely disassociated Rachel from a kidnapper. "Thanks, but I'll call a cab," she said, eager to get home and share the news—and the cheque—with Gran.

CASEY SUCKED IN her breath when Gran held the cheque up to the kitchen light. "Careful."

"Don't worry, it won't catch on fire." Gran squinted at it and mumbled, "One, two, three, four. Huh." She lowered the cheque and handed it back to Casey. "Definitely four zeroes."

"Can you believe it? I've made more than I would have made working at Walmart for the same time period. I can do this! Okay, I need more clients, and now that I've closed my case, I suppose I'm technically unemployed again . . ."

"And that ten grand won't go very far. You have to buy a bike, pay taxes, invest some into promoting your business . . . and I've been giving you a break on the rent."

"Yeah," Casey said mournfully. Amazing how quickly ten thousand dollars could shrink.

Gran nudged her arm. "Don't worry about catching up on the rent for now. Hell, I see it as me investing in you, and you haven't disappointed. I'm proud of you."

Casey's vision blurred. "Really?"

"Really. You're the first business owner in our family. That's quite the accomplishment."

"Aw, thanks, Gran." Casey rose from the kitchen chair to hug her. "I'll find more clients."

"I know you will," Gran said, patting Casey's back. "Use some of that money to buy yourself business cards. You keep talking about them."

"I'll order some tomorrow," Casey promised.

"So everything went okay tonight?" Gran asked when they parted.

"Apart from that freak accident in the parking lot that took out the bike rack, it went like clockwork." Casey tucked the cheque back into her pocket. Sleeping with it under her pillow wouldn't be a good idea; she'd slip it into her desk drawer. "Yep, went off without a hitch. No problems whatsoever."

Her phone rang. She pulled it out and smiled. "Hi."

"Hi," Emily said. "I said I'd call. But . . . well, I'm outside your building. Do you want to come down and chat for a few minutes?"

"Sure! I'll be there in a couple." She hung up. "Emily's downstairs. I'm just going to go talk to her for a bit."

"You should have invited her up."

Casey stifled a snort. That would have been cozy, her, Emily—and Gran. "Nah, she's not staying long. I guess she just wants to see for herself that I'm okay."

Gran's forehead creased. "Poor mite. She must have been worried about how you were getting on, like I was."

"She was definitely worried." To the point of taking action. You know, that was kind of cool. Emily hadn't sat at home and fretted; she'd taken matters into her own hands. "The more I get to know her, the more I like her."

"You're smitten," Gran stated.

Casey surrendered. "Yeah, I am." Hopefully she hadn't just jinxed her fledgling relationship with Emily. "I should go, or she'll wonder if I'm coming down."

"Go, go," Gran said, shooing her out.

Casey made a detour to the bedroom to store away the precious cheque, then raced from the apartment. The elevator took forever to arrive, and the ride down dragged, too. Swinging the lobby door open, Casey took a deep breath and searched for Emily's car. She had to force herself to walk slowly when she spotted Emily leaning against it.

"I know it's almost eleven," Emily said.

"Who cares? You were going to call me. Seeing you is a bonus."

Emily's cheeks reddened. She cleared her throat.

"Did the cops give you any trouble?"

"No. I got the," she lowered her voice and spoke gruffly, "'that's a reckless thing you did, young lady,' speech."

"It *was* reckless . . . and totally awesome! You swooped in and rescued me, just like Wonder Woman!"

"That's the nicest thing anyone's ever said to me," Emily said, her eyes glistening.

Casey's throat tightened. "If I sounded ungrateful, I'm sorry."

"Don't worry about it. I suppose I could have told you I planned to be there. I'll do that next time."

Next time? "Um . . ."

Emily pushed away from the car. "Anyway, I figured I'd take my chances and show up, rather than call, so we can pick up where we left off."

"Where we left off . . ."

Emily waggled her eyebrows. "I know we're not in the back seat of a police car."

Walker yanking the back door open came rushing back. Ah. "This will more than do." Casey took Emily's face in her hands and gently touched her lips to Emily's. Then she closed her eyes and lost herself to the moment. For Casey Cook, private investigator, life was looking up.

Other titles by Sarah Ettritch

Threaded Through Time
The Salbine Sisters
The Rymellan Series
The Deiform Fellowship Series

If you'd like to be notified when Sarah releases a new book, sign up for the notification list at her website: www.sarahettritch.com.

Thanks for reading!